THE LIBRARY LADIES AND THE BODY BEHIND THE LIBRARY

THE LIBRARY LADIES AND THE BODY BEHIND THE LIBRARY

MARIE GREEN

authorHOUSE®

AuthorHouse™
1663 Liberty Drive
Bloomington, IN 47403
www.authorhouse.com
Phone: 1-800-839-8640

Published by AuthorHouse   11/09/2012

ISBN: 978-1-4772-4586-6 (sc)
ISBN: 978-1-4772-4587-3 (hc)
ISBN: 978-1-4772-4588-0 (e)

Thanks a million to Ashlea, Daniel and Gary for helping me get to the finished article; thanks to Bev for giving me the idea to write about the library ladies rather than just talk about them and thanks to Merch for being my soulmate.

CHAPTER ONE

The other library ladies looked expectantly at Matilda in silence, waiting "I . . . I'm just not sure" she mumbled shaking her head slowly, the look on her face demonstrated how conflicted she was. Steph looked around the cosy living room and rolled her eyes, this had been going on for nearly ten minutes and her patience was wearing thin; this had to be a record even for Matilda. "Look Matilda, it shouldn't be this difficult. We're ordering pizza, chips, salad and some cheesy garlic bread; why don't you just share those?" her frustration and rumbling stomach were making her a little tetchy. "Oh no" Matilda frowned and puckered up her lips, which with her head leaning slightly forward on her neck gave her the appearance of a wise turtle. "You know." she looked down at her stomach and mysteriously patted it as it rested gently on the waistband of her flowery skirt. The others didn't really know what she meant when she did that, but it was clearly an important and secretive gesture, so they never dared question it.

"No, I have to be so careful about what I eat. Right, I definitely want haddock, I think I had cod last time—yes, haddock and can I have a few of your chips, I won't eat a whole portion".

Rosie leaned over to Marie "Its enough to drive us all to drink! I'm bloody starving—how hard can a choice between two things be?" She whispered conspiratorially then jumped up and skipped into the kitchen to use the phone. Marie lifted the peach Lambrini and waggled the bottle invitingly; "Anyone for a top up?" Steph smiled and waved her glass hopefully at Marie who filled her glass up then her own.

"I'm walking home anyway. It would have been madness to drive in this snow when I live so close—Merch is going to walk down to meet me when we're finished".

Marie only lived about a quarter of a mile away, although it was up quite a steep hill and across the busy Bristol Road. If the weather was bad—actually or good, she walked so she could have a drink and not be tempted to drive. Rosie's head popped round the door with the phone pressed against her ear, "Matilda, they haven't got any haddock—is cod ok?" Matilda looked up and smiled "Of course dear, I prefer cod anyway, haddock gives me wind"—the rest of the library ladies tried unsuccessfully to suppress a collective giggle.

Wendy coughed to try and distract Matilda and gave the others a stern look. "How's Gerald these days Matilda?" Matilda put a serious face on "Well, ever since that incident in Egypt, he has been a bit over protective to be honest. He drops me off everywhere, keeps calling me on the phone and arrives everywhere early to pick me up, then he moans because he has to wait. It's wearing me out to be honest." The incident in Egypt Matilda was referring to was on their last holiday; Gerald had got 'Egyptian tummy' from some dodgy fish dish during their trip down the Nile and had to spend a day in the hotel room (mostly in the bathroom apparently). Matilda, not wanting to waste a whole warm sunny day, decided to go for a walk in the streets around the hotel. During her wandering she met a 'lovely young man' called Omar and got chatting to him as she often did due to her being extremely friendly and eternally innocent. He asked if she would like to go with him into the desert on his camel and meet his teenage wife.

Instead of politely telling him that at seventy four she shouldn't really be heading into the desert on the back of a camel with a complete stranger; especially as no one would know where she was, she said yes, she would love to go.

Apparently she had a lovely day with Omar and his fourteen year old pregnant wife, Nayna only drawing the line at having dinner in their tent with them, and this only because she could actually see creatures going into and coming back out of the pot. Omar brought Matilda safely back and she gave him her watch for his trouble (she had lost her purse mysteriously during the trip) and went back to tell Gerald what a lovely day she had had.

Gerald however wasn't in a very receptive mood, he had called the police two hours before Matilda returned as it was getting dark and he had no idea what had happened to her. Apparently he got in quite a lot of trouble for wasting police time although luckily they had managed to stop the broadcasting of the police interview on TV before it went out. However it was made clear to both of them that they should avoid holidaying in Egypt for quite a while.

Matilda was baffled by the whole thing; she never considered that Gerald would be worried about where she was. He was trapped in the hotel bathroom wrapped in the complimentary bath robe emptying his body of all fluids into the sink, the bidet or the toilet when she left. She thought he would be fully entertained with those activities all day; she found an English channel for him on the telly and never gave him another thought. She hadn't realised however that she had been gone for over six hours.

"Other than that he's fine, he bought a metal detector and is determinedly searching Bewdly for ancient coins and artefacts. No luck so far though, he did find what he thought was some kind of old boomerang type weapon, but it turned out to be a rusty bottom suspension arm from an old mini—still a collectors piece, but not really valuable—luckily enough James (their son) saw it and recognised what it was before Gerald managed to get it on Ebay"

Just then, Rosie came back in to collect the cash for the food, "£4.50 each will leave £1.30 for the tip—is that enough do you think?" She looked hopeful. "Don't be so mean—on a miserable night like this we should give them a bigger tip than that" said Wendy. "How about, 'get a job that means you don't have to drive about with other peoples food all night' for a tip?" mumbled Marie; Rosie gave her a shove which created a comic moment as Marie caught Lambrini which shot up in the air from the shove, in her open mouth. "Perhaps we can all put an extra 15p and that gives them £2" Wendy chipped in helpfully. "Yeah if you can't add up" Marie, of course. "Marie stop being so mean, have another drink and chill your beans" says Steph. Marie snorted unattractively "Really Steph? Chill your beans?? You spend too much time with your teenage daughters hun, grown ups don't say that—although I do accept I was being mean—so here's an extra 20p to make up for it" she flicked a twenty pence piece into the money pile. Wendy gave Marie 'the look' which she used to instil fear into her family, with her steely blue eyes and ferocious stare, it may have worked on them but Marie was impervious to it.

"Oh dear" says Steph "he's at it again" and she points out of Rosie's front window. Across the road in the upstairs bedroom, lights on and curtains open, a young man was clearly giving himself some attention (if you know what I mean).

Every now and again he slowed down and glanced across the road at Rosie's house, the front window lit up to the outside world with the curtains open.

It's hard to imagine what he saw in the brightly lit room. Rosie is the youngest at forty; petit with short dark hair rather elfin in appearance and looks considerably younger than she is. She's very pretty in an always in fashion kind of way with deep brown eyes and a generous happy mouth. She takes good care of herself even with the pressures of working full time with two young children and a busy husband working shifts. Marie is next oldest at forty six; with multi coloured hair in an asymmetrical bob, green eyes and an attractive but unremarkable face. She wears fashionable clothing and she also looks younger than her actual age (which she rarely admits anyway) but hers is partially due to her spending too much of her hard earned cash on every new anti aging product on the market and knowing exactly what to wear to make the best of herself.

Steph is forty nine but looks closer to Marie's age if not younger; she is pale with gentle blue eyes and wavy shoulder length naturally blond hair. She wears little or no make up and mostly sticks with classic feminine clothes that flatter her curves. Wendy is sixty two and currently sporting purple streaks in her white hair. She is definitely more into comfort where clothing is concerned than fashion or a particular style. She has gradually gained weight over the years (as we all do!) but is clinging to her size eighteen with solid determination.

She didn't mind anything about her size other than it sometimes impeded her ability to play with her grandchildren. Finally there is Matilda who is seventy five years young and an undeterminable size in clothing. She has an adventurous nature which plays out in her clothing and choice of hair colour. Sporting a simple bob and a severe fringe for as long as anyone could remember, her hair colour ranges from bright ginger to mahogany brown depending on which hair dye is on special offer when she gets fed up of the bold grey streak at her roots. Technically Matilda is no longer a library lady as she retired about fifteen years ago, but to be honest she is at the library almost as much as she was when she worked there.

They all blatantly stared at the young man fascinated by his shenanigans "I wish I had driven now" Marie said wistfully. The others looked at her perplexed "Oh, it's just that then I'd have my glasses; right now I can't see anything but a fast moving blur"

She sighed loudly and looked genuinely disappointed; Rosie and Steph burst out laughing, Matilda looked blank and Wendy tutted and moved to close the curtains "It's not funny, we shouldn't encourage him, I've a good mind to go over there and tell his mother",

"I wouldn't if I was you Wendy" cautioned Rosie "she's a bit of a livewire to say the least. She got into a fight with the dustbin man on Tuesday and they had to call the police to get her off him. She was trying to post him into the back of his own truck! All because he wouldn't take her paper for recycling cos she had some cardboard in the recycling box—the whole thing was bonkers. It seemed to go on for ages and not one person went out to stop it." She shook her head sadly as if disappointed in her neighbours.

She looked around at the others who were all now looking at her questioningly "Obviously I would have" she sounded a bit defensive now "but I was in the middle of making cup cakes for a wedding on Saturday. I burnt one set anyway watching the fight; she was vicious, really scary and a proper potty mouth, I had to turn up Peppa Pig so that Lucy and Billy didn't hear her. They're very funny at nursery when they use that kind of language. Very judgemental actually." She went a bit red as if she had a story to tell but when Marie's eyebrows went up she mumbled something about hearing the pizza delivery man and picked up the cash to go to the door and collect their food.

She arrived back laden with boxes and bags of fabulously smelling food and there then followed ten minutes of solid eating—sharing out of pizza, digging in to chips ripping up cheesy garlic bread and ignoring salad. "Chilli flakes anyone" chirped Rosie "Rather have tomato sauce please" Marie squeezed out through a mouthful of food, trying not to spray anything out of her mouth back into the pizza boxes.

The food was all laid out like a carpet picnic on the oriental style rug with the ladies seated on the floor around it to allow easy access. (Except Matilda who sat on the settee as she had said on many occasions that she wouldn't be able to get back up if she sat on the floor). The ladies sat munching happily in a general mess of noise and smells.

Rosie's house was warm and welcoming with a mix of family memories, photographs and unusual ornaments like angels and gargoyles picked up from various holidays.

The huge television dominated the front room which was the favourite room for library ladies night. They obviously never had it on once Rosie's two small children had gone to bed, but Rosie said it was an essential with small children. She lived on quite a busy tree lined road, busy during the day anyway. There was even a small bus that used it, which drove Rosie mad (unless she had to use it) but by the evening it was mostly quiet so it was a lovely homely room for the old friends to relax in.

For a few minutes Matilda was completely silent; no one enjoys unhealthy food night as much as she does as normally she is a very healthy eater (or so she tells everyone, evidence of Matilda's healthy eating is scant). But she throws herself into library lady night with gusto only previously demonstrated when visiting Cadbury World. Gerald said she ate so many of the free samples she had to spend quite a long time in the toilet, causing a considerable queue of desperate little girls, particularly as the other one of the two toilets was broken which only left one for public use. After around twenty minutes Matilda was finished and as she left the toilet she explained to the waiting crowd of moms and children that she had a 'serious complaint' which meant she had to relax for a while before she could 'go'. If they hadn't been able to hear her retching, they might have forgiven her.

"Shall I finish those chips so they don't go to waste?" she asked the room generally "Fill your boots" said Marie through half munched pizza; she watched a lot of American sit coms and prides herself in finding the appropriate times to insert these random comments, unfortunately Matilda takes it all rather literally and looked confused "No thank you dear, I'll just eat them here, they go soggy if you try to reheat them."

She then polished off the chips, the last of the pizza and only missed the cheesy garlic bread by a millisecond; Rosie saw her looking at the last piece and swooped down on it with surprising speed. "Anyone want some of this salad?" offers Steph pointlessly, they always end up with salad left over.

"Not for me" says Matilda "I have to be careful about how much I eat" she patted her expanding tummy again. Everyone else shares a secret smile and Rosie, collecting up the empty boxes and cartons said "Well I hope you've saved some space for a bit of pudding because I have been baking today". She wandered out to the kitchen with the food debris balanced on the biggest empty pizza box. Moments later she returned with some lovely looking cup cakes on a pretty china plate. It was always a treat when library lady night was at Rosie's because she loved baking and tested all her new flavours out on the others. They all took one and bit into the soft warm cakes "well?" she said looking around expectantly "Mmm" said Marie "I can't quite identify the kick of flavour after the vanillary taste—what is it?"

Rosie looked triumphant "Sprouts!" she announced "What do you think? I thought it could really catch on. It's a great way to get unpopular vegetables into kids don't you think? All about your five a day—works for carrots, carrot cake is very popular." Her enthusiasm was tangible.

Matilda started to cough into her serviette and Wendy shot upstairs saying she needed a wee but Marie smiled approvingly "Mmm I still like it. Just a little bit worried about the wind afterwards, sprouts are always a problem for me, they're worse than beans". Rosie looked pleased with herself and turned to Steph for her reaction.

Steph was obviously carefully framing what she wanted to say, "Well I'm not absolutely convinced that sprout cake will take off in the baking world if I'm being honest. The bits of leaf are a bit off-putting, and to be frank the flavour is a bit, well, odd. But I think it is admirable that you are still testing out lots of flavours—my favourite is still the parsnip sponge, but you never know, those vegetarian type parents might pay for them." Steph smiled reassuringly at Rosie who wasn't sure how to take what Steph had said "I'm a vegetarian parent myself?" she said. "There you go then" said Steph as if she had proven a valid point.

Just then Wendy came back in looking a bit sheepish "Honestly, I loved the cake" she effused as she plonked back down on the comfy sofa. "I just really needed a wee. It's the cold you know, can't hold it like I used to." Rosie held up the plate "Would anyone like another one?" She invited temptingly. A resounding "No" came a bit too quickly from everyone except Marie who lit up. "Yes please. Got any cream or custard?" Rosie shook her head. "Don't you mean gravy?" whispered Wendy and Steph giggled.

"Anyway" said Matilda as if she was making an announcement "I saw the library ghost again on Wednesday. I was in the staff room resting my eyes while I waited for the kettle to boil and I sensed someone there. At first I thought it was Wendy coming in for her break, but when I opened my eyes I saw it was a man. He was kind of shimmery and not all there, you know—a bit see through. I closed my eyes again and cleaned my glasses on my skirt, but when I looked back at him, he was still there. Just standing still and he was looking right at me.

I tried to act casual and I said "you can't come in here sir, its staff only" but he carried on looking at me as if he didn't hear what I said. Then, just as I managed to get the courage to stand up, he pointed at the back wall of the library and walked right through it! I was quite shaken up, I had to have sugar in my tea didn't I Wendy?" Wendy nodded in confirmation (of the sugar not the ghost). "Did you recognise him?" Marie asked. Matilda shook her head "No, never seen him before. He was just an ordinary looking man in his fifty's, not much hair left, trousers and a shirt and he wore glasses."

Rosie looked questioningly at Marie, and without actually saying 'you surely don't believe this?' it was written all over her face, Marie shrugged.

Wendy spoke quietly as if the ghost might hear "Perhaps we should have the vicar come down—hey Rosie how about Helen coming in and exercising the library?" Rosie's sister had recently qualified as a vicar, "It's exorcising not exercising and I'm not asking her, she would think I was barmy. Matilda are you sure you hadn't been drinking or had you dropped off to sleep in there? There has to be a reasonable explanation." Matilda looked at Rosie as if she was a bit simple "Rosie, I was wide awake and I haven't drunk alcohol since that nasty experience in Turkey in 1994, so clearly I was sober. Why do you find it so hard to believe it is a ghost?" Rosie looked sincere. "Because I don't believe in ghosts, that's why. They don't make sense so I am just trying to find a logical explanation for what you think you saw" she looked uncomfortable to be the centre of the discussion.

"Well" said Matilda "don't waste your time and energy Rosie, it was a ghost and nothing you say will convince me otherwise. I have seen him three times now; always on a Wednesday afternoon during my break after the readers club".

"Aha" says Steph dramatically "There it is then; that's our way to establish if the ghost is real. Tomorrow is Wednesday, instead of having the day off; we can all go to the library and wait to see if Matilda's ghost appears."

Matilda looked indulgently at Steph "Really dear, it's not my ghost, I just see it. But that is quite a good idea—perhaps you lot can help me work out what he's trying to say because I can't seem to figure it out on my own".

Rosie didn't look happy "I have tap class with Lucy and Billy after school on Wednesdays." She looked a bit sheepish and was wriggling about on the settee.

"You're scared!" pronounced Marie enthusiastically "that's what it is you girlie! Matilda, what time do you see your ghost?" "Not my ghost dear, as I said to Steph, just a ghost. It's about break time, so that's three ish" Marie grinned at Rosie mischievously "Your tap class doesn't start until four, so you can easily make it to the ghost club first, shake hands with Gregor the ghost and head up for the little darlings." Rosie scowled at Marie but admitted defeat "Alright then, I will come, but just to prove that ghosts don't exist when nothing happens. No offence Matilda but you know what you're like after lunch. You fell asleep while actually reading a story to the readers club only last month." Matilda looked affronted and went a bit pink "I had been sleeping very badly that week actually Rosie; Gerald had such a cold and he was snoring like a warthog, even with a scarf wrapped round my head I could hear him.

I was exhausted and it was so warm and quiet in the library, at least two of the readers club were already asleep. I paused in the story for effect and before I knew it I was toppling off the chair; embarrassing really, lucky I had trousers on." Wendy patted Matilda's shoulder as reassurance and gave Rosie the look; Rosie raised her eyebrows and shrugged as if to say 'what?? It happened'.

"Ok folks, its ten o'clock and I am going to hit the road. I've text Merch and he is slipping and sliding his way down to meet me as we speak. I will meet you all at the library at one thirty tomorrow, that should give us time for a cuppa before we start our ghost hunting."

Marie was clearly enjoying the whole thing—possibly because she had drunk nearly a full bottle of peach lambrini and a glass of sherry. She happily collected her things, wrapped herself in her warm coat and scarf and kissed everyone goodbye.

She found the walk home in the snow exhilarating and a great way to use up some of the calories she had consumed during the night. She loved the idea of ghost hunting at the library, very exciting so she gave herself a little hug. Nothing interesting ever happened to her so things were definitely looking up and the journey flew by with daydreams of ghost busting and daring dos.

She was nearly home by the time she realised she had somehow missed Merch. She wasn't quite so exhilarated when she had to walk back down the road to find him. She was even less exhilarated when she had to walk back again to the sound of him explaining where the instructions she had given him on where they were to meet were faulty.

By the time she got home she had a headache a freezing cold nose and ears and was already regretting giving up half of her day off to go and wait for a non existent ghost in the library where she already spent five days a week. Oh well she had said she would now, so that was that. She arrived home tired and cold and feeling very much like going to bed without any further conversation, so she made tea for Merch and a cup of hot chocolate for herself and kindle in hand, she headed for a nice warm bed.

Once everyone had left Rosie found it hard to settle down; Lucy and Billy her two lively children were fast asleep and Mick, her paramedic husband, was on a night shift, so she had the house to herself.

She wasn't quite as sure as she had said to the others that ghosts were non existent. She had never seen a ghost herself and she was glad about that, but some of her most credible friends had said they had and just the thought of it scared her silly. She felt a shiver go through her and she could have sworn she heard the kitchen door opening. She held her breath and listened for a minute unmoving—nothing.

She peeped out of the living room door to see if anything was there, at the same time praying that it was just the wind or her imagination. Still nothing, the door was half open and creaking, but no ghostly apparition floated out of the kitchen.

She dashed out into the hall and shut the door with a bang, demonstrating to the empty house that she was not afraid. Then she ran upstairs to bed, leaving all the lights on. She quickly washed and changed into her sensible pyjamas for bed.

She lay awake unable to fall asleep regretting washing the lambrini down with sherry and wishing desperately that she had said she was busy tomorrow afternoon.

Steph loved the drama of the ghost in the library. She drove home very slowly in the snow, imagining the ghost appearing and the pandemonium with her friends all being terrified. In her imagination she was the one calming everyone down and communicating calmly with the ghost to establish why it was haunting the library and comforting her friends bravely. She was so carried away with her day dreaming that she forgot to be scared about driving in the snow and arrived home safely with her car and confidence intact.

After sliding carefully up the drive, she put her key in the lock and listened to the house, out of habit before pushing the door open. She was waiting for the shouting, screaming or loud music associated with three teenage daughters but the house was silent. She frowned mystified as she walked through the dark hall to the large modern kitchen where she found a note from Nigel balanced on the black marble counter by the kettle. 'Me and the girls have gone out for a drink and some grub, see you later'. Steph physically relaxed letting out a breath she didn't know she was holding, quiet and calm for a while longer.

She made herself a cup of tea and picked up her book, bed and solitude—a rare pleasure in Steph's world and she was not going to waste one single minute. She climbed into her pyjamas, all thoughts of ghosts forgotten and opened her book about vampires and werewolves and passion and love and started to disappear into their world.

Gerald was waiting outside Rosie's house in his car with the engine running for Matilda. She was supposed to be out at ten o'clock but her watch had stopped the day before and she had forgotten to wind it up. Once Marie had gone, she just had to pop to the loo then get her boots and everything on and before she knew it, she was late. When she climbed into the nice warm car, Gerald began lecturing her about how important it was to keep to a timetable to ensure they had structure and were able to fit everything in to their busy lives. Matilda wanted to say that at quarter past ten at night there is nothing else to fit in except bed, but as Gerald had been good enough to come and pick her up in the snow, she kept quiet.

They got home in about twenty minutes; it is only a five minute journey, but because of the snow and Gerald being extra careful, even more careful than usual (although that is only just possible whilst maintaining any kind of actual motion) it took much longer.

The house was lovely and warm and enveloped her as she walked in. Earlier in the week Gerald had turned the thermostat down on the central heating because he said it is more economical to have a constant heat rather than hot then cold. But Matilda had turned it back up when he fell asleep in his chair. Matilda didn't like the cold, it made her ankles ache, even if she wore socks, so she wanted the heat up all the time in the winter and Gerald was forgetful enough to not notice.

Matilda put milk on the hob for their hot chocolate and Gerald went into the living room to sit in his favourite chair and read his paper (again). "How were the girls tonight then Matilda?" he called.

Matilda walked in with the cups of hot chocolate on a small tray. "Oh those girls are lovely and funny too, always something to make you smile, although to be fair I only understand half what they're talking about. Here I brought you a cup cake that Rosie made" Gerald looked a bit concerned as he took the cake from Matilda.

"Oh I'm not sure about Rosie's cakes, no offence but didn't the last one have swede in it? Made me feel sick the thought of vegetables in cakes" He made a face to emphasise how bizarre he thought it was. "You like carrot cake" said Matilda matter of factly, "Yes, but that doesn't actually have carrot in does it—its just called carrot cake". Matilda looked at Gerald to see if he was teasing, but he looked serious, Matilda shook her head bewildered "Gerald, carrot cakes do have carrots in them" Gerald bit the cake and chewed slowly as if he was waiting for it to bite him back. "Matilda, this tastes a bit strange and I think there is paper in it? I don't think I want it, did you say there is carrot in it?". "No dear" Matilda said "I said there is carrot in carrot cake. In these cakes there are sprouts and that is what you have in your teeth, not paper." Gerald made a deep growling noise and looked as if he might say something else, but instead he slapped his paper down and stomped off in to the kitchen, where Matilda could hear him gargling.

Oh well, she sighed to herself. She picked up her hot chocolate and leaving him to it she shouted good night and went up to bed. She brushed her hair and gazed in the mirror at her reflection.

She looked a bit pale, perhaps she needed to start wearing make up. She rubbed her cheeks a bit to try and make them rosy like they do in movies, but it didn't work.

She stared into her own big green eyes, perhaps they made her look pale or maybe it was her hair which was still quite dark (chestnut dream). She looked at the face in the mirror; had she seen a ghost? It felt so real when she was there but now it seemed a bit daft. Perhaps she was getting dementia or something and she was imagining things that weren't there? She shook her head at the face in the mirror, oh well tomorrow would tell.

She picked up her cup and climbed into bed, collecting her book about gardening as she leaned back on her pillows and pulled her downy quilt up over her. Just five minutes reading before switching the light off for sleep.

Wendy drove home slowly, carefully steering the car through the snow and around the parked and abandoned cars. She was a confident driver, but she didn't really like driving at night any more. Her eyesight wasn't what it used to be, although she didn't like to admit it, so she was extra careful and was grateful that no one was around to witness her one mile drive home in second gear.

She had a no nonsense approach to any task she undertook and was proud of it. She needed it with three grown up girls and grandchildren all demanding her time and attention. She had to share herself out and not forget Mark, her husband of forty six years.

She mentally shook her head, sometimes she wondered why she came to these library lady nights.

Tonight especially, the weather was filthy and to be honest she thought the others were a bit frivolous. She loved them though in her way; even though they were a bit daft and giggly and said the most irrelevant things. Especially Rosie and Marie; they teased Matilda awfully, although to be fair Matilda rarely noticed. That wasn't the point; it was disrespectful of them to tease someone Matilda's age. She was not sure what to make of Matilda's ghost, she didn't want to outright say that she thought it couldn't be true, but at the same time, she didn't believe in ghosts. It didn't fit with her whole personality or outlook. Still what harm could it do, spending an hour with Matilda and the others at the library just waiting? She was working anyway so she would comfort Matilda afterwards; convince her it was something she ate or a virus or something.

She pulled up outside her house. Mark's car was already on the drive so she blocked him in; she would be off out before him tomorrow. He rarely went out in the morning since he retired, preferring to potter about in the house or garden till he walked up to the local school to pick up Cameron, one of their grandsons, each day.

He felt needed because of this important job and it helped make up for the fact that he had worked every hour he could when they were younger to try and keep his wife and three daughters happy. He walked Cameron to the shops and up to their house to play until Emma; their daughter picked him up when she finished work.

It was good that he had something to do each day—Wendy still worked part time at the library but was counting the days down until she could retire, she couldn't wait.

She walked into the warm open plan lounge where Mark was already coming back in from the kitchen with a cup of tea for her. "Here you go sweetheart, had it all ready for you. I knew you'd be back around now and would like a nice cuppa. Heard the car pull up and jumped to it." Mark had a habit of describing what he did or his thought process out loud. Wendy was used to it by now; she didn't even really notice it anymore. She had loved it when they first got together; she felt like he was trying to help her understand everything he did, like they shared everything. Then after a few years when the children were young, she wanted to smother him with a pillow almost every day!! She was so young herself and always so tired with the children she would look forward to him getting home so she could have an adult conversation.

But he would go on and on and into endless detail of why he had chosen a ham sandwich rather than cheese or describe in detail some other irrelevant decision that she was definitely not interested in. She got to the stage some days where she just wanted to hurt him.

She had managed not to do him any serious harm through those years (although she did throw a dirty nappy and various other articles near to hand at him more than once to try and shut him up) and now she had come full circle and quite enjoyed it again. Strange. People are strange.

She thanked Mark for her drink and sat down in front of the telly sliding her feet into her waiting slippers. She would watch the rest of the news then take her book up to bed with her and get lost in the Victorian beauty and dignity of her current read.

Far more palatable than the world she actually lived in with boys deliberately playing with themselves where respectable women could see and supposed ladies fighting with the bin men—where will it all end?

CHAPTER TWO

T he next day dawned bright and crisp and the low golden sun had managed to thaw much of the snow on the footpaths and roads.

Vehicles moved about more freely, sloshing grey mulch onto the footpaths and up other cars and onto the litter and plants that had been hidden by the snow as they emerged triumphant into sight.

All of the library ladies forgot the ghost initially on waking. Marie stretched out to enjoy her morning off feeling, wishing she had invested in a teasmaid so she didn't have to go downstairs to get a cup of tea. Tea in bed was never as enjoyable if you had to get out of bed to make it yourself. She always ended up staying up and heading into the shower ready to start the day.

The bedroom she and Merch shared was cream and ruby red, very modern but comfortable too and Marie loved waking up in it. She only had to turn her head to see the quiet road outside the front window between the cracks in the curtains. She loved the way the tree directly in front of their house highlighted the seasons; today it was bare, dormant for the winter waiting for spring to come and wake it up.

The house she and Merch lived in was a 1930's semi with a bay window at the front.

She was so proud of it; long gone were the days when the children were young and she lived in a council flat. She loved coming home, pulling up on the drive knowing it was her home, always taking time to check which flowers were out on the walk to the front door and noticing any bulbs that had sent up green shoots. She sat up to look outside and the sharp pain in her temple reminded her of the night before. She remembered she was going into work to witness a ghost visitor and she smiled to herself. A good night's sleep had left her feeling quite refreshed apart from the slight hangover. The extra hour in bed had helped and she decided she didn't need her tea in bed after all. The day held the potential of being very different from the ordinary. She might not have been so optimistic had she known what the day ahead held.

Rosie's morning was much less relaxed than Marie's. Her morning routine mostly entailed retrieving items of food from clothing and items of clothing from hiding places and herding what felt like a flock of children into the car for the day to begin. She took the children to nursery and school without a thought for the afternoon rendezvous. She was distracted more than usual, mainly because Billie had drawn on Lucy with an indelible black marker because she had said she wanted to be a ladybird.

He had very carefully coloured her face with spots and no amount of exfoliating cream had got them completely off. By the time they left the house the face in between the spots was so red, she actually did look a bit like a ladybird.

Rosie dropped Billie off at nursery and Lucy at school. She quickly left the building before the disapproving teachers could give her the look that always made her feel like an incompetent mother.

Steph woke with a start when a loud crash from the kitchen was followed by what sounded like world war breaking out. Nigel had already gone to work so she braced herself to make her way downstairs and try to establish peace with the three beautiful, but volatile daughters who were most likely arguing over who should have what space to prepare their breakfast. She climbed out of bed and grabbed her dressing gown from the en suite. Hugging it to her she wished she had just had ten minutes to wake up properly before needing to call on her natural reserves of patience for the counselling and mediation needed to prevent physical injury to one or more of her daughters.

Matilda spent the early morning collecting items for her reader's club discussion about holidays. She and Gerald had been adventurous over the years and even now in their seventy's they went on holiday at least three times a year and didn't mind camping or youth hostelling if they could get a bargain in an unusual place. She picked up the yellow helmet; this was from last year's holiday in Cumbria; Matilda had gone white water rafting—mainly because she didn't know what it was and there was a space. The lovely young lad who was her instructor said she was the oldest customer he had ever had and he noticed how brave she was, although she was a bit scared half way through. Gerald had taken photographs of flowers; actually she would take those for the readers club too. She sighed satisfied with her haul and went to sit at the dining table ready for her breakfast. Gerald was poaching eggs in their kitchen and the teapot was already on the table under a knitted cosy with a rack of hot toast, Matilda smiled and reached for her cup.

Wendy wasn't that keen on mornings, although she had to admit they were a lot less hectic now the children had all gone. Mark would spend his first waking minutes vocalising what he planned to do for that day and Wendy would lie quietly listening and not really listening. Then some time during the narration she would drift off into wishing it was a non working day (even though because she was part time and only worked three days, it very often was.). Today she was helping Matilda with the readers club; it was a holiday theme so she didn't have anything to take. She hadn't been on holiday for years; she couldn't see the point of them. Spending all that money to sleep in a strange bed in a strange place eating strange food with strangers—no definitely not Wendy's cup of tea.

She was a home body, loved her family fiercely. She was proud of her lovely modern tidy house and liked to be master of all she surveyed. She liked to cook good simple homely food and she loved the children and their families to come round and appreciate it. Wendy adored being a grandmother and took it very seriously; she wished she could dedicate herself to it full time.

So unfortunately she didn't have anything to contribute to the readers club today, she would take their coats, make the refreshments and comment appreciatively when everyone else talked about their holiday mementos.

One thirty on the dot Marie and Rosie met outside the library; Wendy and Matilda were already inside and their cars were parked outside but no sign of Steph yet.

"I don't feel any better about this today, I haven't got time to be messing about with ghost busting, and I need to be doing some housework!" Rosie whined.

Marie smiled at her "Come on honey, what harm can it do? You said you don't believe in ghosts and I certainly don't, so it will just be a bit of a laugh, no harm done and we'll be out by half three. And don't pretend you would have been doing housework, because you would have been watching Loose Women and some other daytime drivel. We are probably doing you a massive favour keeping you away from discovering the latest trend or fashion item that you couldn't afford anyway". Rosie grinned lightening up "You know me too well, and I know you would be doing the same." "Correct" concurred Marie with a decisive nod, "but I wasn't pretending that I would be doing housework—I definitely wouldn't be. I might be painting my nails, reading a book, drawing a picture or shopping, but I definitely wouldn't be doing any kind of housework. I ban housework on a day off midweek, Sunday morning is housework time and no other day shall be tainted by it!" She hooked her arm in Rosie's and they marched up the steps and got to the door just as Steph pulled up.

"Hang on" Steph shouted hurriedly her head out of her car window "I can't find my key, so wait for me will you; I'll come in with you two". She disappeared back into the car, hurriedly grabbed her huge handbag, a random carrier bag, which appeared to be empty and tumbled backwards out of the car on to the pavement. She ran up the steps as if she was being chased. "Are you ok hun" Rosie asked. "Oh yes thanks, just running a bit behind. Gilly had a row with Eugenie and cut up her favourite Villa scarf and when Bella tried to calm them down they both turned on her and accidentally cut some of her hair off" Steph tried a strained smile and rolled her eyes exasperatingly.

Her girls were very high spirited and completely the opposite of Steph who was mild natured and avoided conflict when ever she could, preferring to mediate and to leave everyone happy. Unfortunately the girls got their temperament somewhere else in the family tree because they preferred to fight to sort issues out and didn't care who got caught in the crossfire.

Steph had a really tough time of it when the girls were in High School, but it had calmed down now they were a little older; only really causing issues when they were all in at the same time. Unfortunately none of them appeared to have any intention of moving out, so respite for Steph was always short lived. Marie and Rosie took an arm each and walked with Steph into the library. They didn't say anything because they knew nothing they said would make it better. Best thing was to make Steph a nice cup of tea and start working to take her mind off her volatile and demanding family.

The readers club were in full swing when they got inside so they had to be quiet. Beryl Burnside was engrossed in her description of the massage she had at the Turkish bath she'd visited whilst in Marmaris last year and her facial expressions and hand movements had the whole club transfixed. No one noticed the other library ladies arrive so they crept into the staff room at the back of the building.

It was a rather cramped room, in keeping with the whole library really. It was a prefab building that had been put up thirty years before as a temporary building supposedly with a life of ten years until the council built a permanent one. Of course they never found the money, so here it stayed.

The bit of space laughingly called the staff room was actually just big enough for a coffee table and two chairs outside a cubby hole that they called the kitchen. Sparsely equipped it contained a sink and a cupboard, a length of kitchen work surface precariously fixed between them which held a kettle and a mug rack full of everyone's favourite mugs. The microwave and toaster sat on the cupboard and the small fridge wedged under the work surface and mostly everyone was happy with it. Mainly anyway, the only problem was caused when more than two people had their break or lunch together. Not all three or more people could sit down at the same time and only one person could fit in the kitchen. For the most part the staff brought sandwiches so there was no trouble at lunchtime. However, if toast was on the menu, it could be bedlam requiring a strict rota to ensure no one went hungry. One wall was entirely covered in racking which held all manner of sparkly material. Sticky back paper, paints, pens, pencils, pots, scissors, scraps of material and everything needed to hold craft sessions for small children. It also allowed the staff to express themselves creatively whenever it was time to do a display for, book week, Christmas, Chinese New Year, no smoking week and so on.

This storage also caused an issue occasionally. The boxes were balanced precariously on the racking and sporadically fell off for no reason. Many a near miss creating big mess in a small place had delayed the opening of the library after lunch (much to the consternation of the line of pensioners waiting to get in).

The gang crowded in and Wendy, who was sitting on one of the chairs, shushed them.

"Try not to get too loud, they are really enjoying themselves today, although to be honest some of the stories they're sharing are a bit inappropriate.

The one Margaret just told about her and the coach driver on her Saga holiday in Benidorm was positively blue! I'm glad most of them have forgotten their hearing aids; Matilda definitely needs to make it clearer that the stories can't be pornographic! She needs to give them some sort of guidelines. Some of those people have weak hearts for goodness sake!" She shook her head exasperatedly. Marie piped up "I have a better idea; why don't we video it, we could make a fortune on You Tube with these oldies talking dirty!"

Rosie giggled but Wendy and Steph gave Marie the look "Trust you to try and think of a way to commercialise the readers club, is nothing sacrilege?" pleaded Wendy despairingly.

"Nope" says Marie "survival of the most commercial means we have to find a way to make money in the library services if we don't want them to privatize us or shut us down. People don't appreciate free stuff and that would be a great way to promote the readers club and make a profit. Alternatively we could keep a camcorder permanently on Matilda and send off weekly clips to You've Been Framed". Even Wendy smiled at that one "She is funny without knowing it. My favourite Matilda incident was when she was too hot at the readers club last summer and took her jumper off forgetting that she didn't have a blouse underneath! I thought Bertie Brown was going to have a heart attack and his wife didn't speak to Matilda for a few weeks. Poor Matilda, she's so sweet, but unfortunate and unbelievable things always happen to her. Take this whole ghost thing. None of you can really believe that the library is haunted and that Matilda saw a ghost? We are surely just humouring her aren't we? It's just I am a bit worried about how she'll take it when nothing happens." Wendy looked concerned. The others had the good grace to look abashed.

Steph shook her head slowly "I'm not completely writing it off as fiction. Some of Matilda's most bonkers stories have turned out to be true. Remember when she was working in the prison library when she first retired and she said a prisoner had got hold of a white coat and spent the day in the library with her, he convinced her that he was a doctor, ordering all sorts of biology books? We all thought that was a tall tale, but it wasn't. It was in the local papers the next week and it turned out the prisoner was armed with a home made shank and certified criminally insane. The only reason he had been left with Matilda so long was they were waiting for the armed response unit to get to the prison to rescue her. She didn't realise the enormity of the whole incident and even after I showed her the paper, she said what a nice lad he was and that she simply didn't believe he killed both his parents and the neighbours. So if I'm honest, I am keeping an open mind until this afternoon proves one way or the other."

The story created a reflective air in the room. Steph was right; some of Matilda's stories in the past had been stranger than fiction.

They were all so used to Matilda's yarns that no one bothered to sort the fiction from non fiction any more—shocking for library staff really, with classification being so important for the books. They all stood thinking about the most ridiculous story Matilda had told that stuck in their minds and they realised that this ghost one wasn't the strangest!

They became very quiet until Matilda came crashing into the staff room with two boxes overflowing with strange items from stockings to stones. "Ooh that went very well." She enthused "took a bit of time to calm Mr Richards down after Mrs Burnsides graphic description of her Turkish massage and how it made her feel, but all in all a very successful afternoon. Now who's putting the kettle on I'm parched?" She did her comic eyebrows and stuck her tongue out to show how parched she was.

Wendy got up to do tea duty and Matilda started categorising the items in the box and tutting at the things that she should have given back to the people in the readers club but forgot. She found a new box and labelled it 'items to return to the readers club'. By the time she had sorted out the original box, the new box was almost full.

She patted her hair "What am I like, so forgetful nowadays." She looked up as if she had just noticed the other's there. "Now what are you lot up to?" she queried. Wendy passed her a mug of tea and started giving everyone else one while Steph reminded Matilda. "We're here to see your ghost Matilda remember? You told us about him last night and we said we would come down to see if he appears again today" Matilda nodded slowly "Oh yes I remember now, although I have said he is not my ghost dear, just a ghost. I don't really want to be closely associated with the spiritual world, Gerald wouldn't like it. What time is it girls, my watch appears to have stopped?" She demonstrated the ineffective watch by listening to it closely to her ear, tapping it and putting her hands out as if she was showing a child that the sweets have all gone. "Quarter to three" said Marie. "Perfect" said Matilda "just time for a wee" and off she shot down the tiny corridor to the toilet.

"She doesn't seem very concerned that we may all be about to see an apparition in a very confined space" puzzled Rosie. "Well" said Steph "she wasn't that afraid when she saw him three times when she was on her own, so I don't suppose seeing him with all of us here will be as unnerving for Matilda. Wendy, what do you think about all this? You were here last time she saw him?" Wendy pulled an awkward face, squashing her lips up like she was reluctant to answer, but everyone looked at her and waited. "Well, she was quite shaken when I came in for my break last week, but to be honest I had peeped through the window about fifteen minutes before and she did look like she was asleep". Rosie looked decidedly relieved "There you go, this is a complete waste of time. I could be sitting happily with a bag of Revels picking up fashion and beauty tips from Loose Women!" She sounded as if she was fed up, but she looked happier than she had since the ghost conversation started the night before; she took a sip of her tea and looked around the room for a biscuit.

There was a crash from the toilet and everyone looked in that direction. They heard Matilda mumble 'bloody mop bucket', but as the group looked at the door Matilda was about to come through, something strange happened. Where Matilda should by rights be entering, there was a vague impression of a man.

No one spoke as Matilda came clambering through the shimmery man trying to wipe her hands on a tea towel. "There's no hand towels left in the toilet and the cleaner left the mop bucket right in the middle of the cupboard they're kept in, I nearly poked my own eye out with the mop handle." She noticed the group were very quiet and staring at her "What? What's wrong?"

Wendy leaned forward to gently take Matilda's hand and guide her away from where she appeared to be standing in the middle of the ghostly man.

Still not a word was uttered but Matilda turned to where they were all looking "Ah there you are, I told you!" She turned round victoriously to look at the others. "Come on feller, speak or something so we can work out what you're trying to say to us".

The others were aghast that Matilda was chatting so openly to a ghost, although it didn't appear to bother the ghost who didn't do or say anything, just hovered there in the doorway. Steph leant over towards Marie and whispered "I know who he is! He's on the supply pool at Northfield library, his name's Barry something. He came here to cover when you were on holiday and Wendy was on a day off. He was quite nice actually. I didn't know he was dead, I wonder what he wants with us?" Right on cue the ghostly man pointed to the back wall of the staff room and floated right through it.

Everyone was totally silent; Rosie and Marie were shaking and had to sit rather quickly on the two available chairs—so much for their bravado and cheek thought Matilda. Wendy cleared a space on the coffee table and sat in it "Well I never" she said "I never thought it was true for a minute, but he was a definite ghost and he did exactly what Matilda said he did. Pass me my tea Steph and put me an extra sugar in it or I might not be able to stand back up" Steph did as she was told and passed the drink to Wendy then went to retrieve her own.

Her hand was shaking but she felt exhilarated! At last a real life adventure and she knew him, she knew the ghost—well the man that he was before he was a ghost.

She leapt into action "Right someone phone Northfield Library and ask what his last name was and what happened to him; speak to Linda, if anyone there knows anything it will be her." Marie automatically moved quickly into the office to do as she was told. "Now, what was he trying to tell us and why is he here? If he was going to haunt a library, surely it would be Northfield, not West Heath. He only came here twice and he seemed to have a nice time. I got chatting to him both times and I definitely got the impression that he offered to come the second time cos he liked it so much the first time. Why would he want to haunt us and what was he trying to tell us?"

They were all considering this question when Marie came back into the room "You are not going to believe this. Linda said they haven't seen him for nearly four weeks; he was supposed to cover here three weeks ago yesterday and he never turned up. As soon as she checked the rota I remembered. We thought Northfield had forgotten to send cover and when I phoned them, the new girl answered and she didn't know what I was talking about so I cancelled the school visit and we got on with the day a person short. But apparently he said to Linda on the Monday night 'see you Thursday Lin, I'm at West Heath tomorrow and off Wednesday' but he never came back. The powers that be have tried contacting his home, wrote to him, and phoned him but got no response. Linda said that because there aren't any suspicious circumstances no one has reported it to the police—they've only gone down the disciplinary route—he is about to get sacked!!"

"Well isn't that just typical" stormed Rosie red faced with indignation "No suspicious circumstances? What do they call disappearing into thin air for goodness sake? What do they call suspicious?

Do we have to send his ghost up to central library to report himself missing? Does this poor guy have no one who has missed him? No family or friends? What kind of a world is this that a man can be missing for nearly four weeks and the only reason anyone notices is because his ghost starts haunting some random work colleagues he barely knows!" Rosie looked like she might be about to cry at the sad situation. "That poor man" crooned Wendy forlornly "we have to find out what happened to him—he must be trying to tell us something. Perhaps he wants us to follow him?" she looked doubtfully at the others. "Really? Through the wall?" Sarcasm as usual from Marie.

"No time for your lip—Not through the wall silly girl, but what's behind that wall?" Wendy asked interested. Matilda perked up a bit, spotting an opportunity to shine for a while "Oh that's easy, nothing is behind this wall" she proclaimed triumphantly. "Nothing? There has to be something, what do you mean by nothing?" quizzed Wendy, everyone looked at Matilda expectantly "Oh well, a space is what I meant by nothing. It used to be called an access alley, but they put a bit of fence on each end years ago to stop the kids getting behind there and causing mayhem for the old librarian. It's all brambles and weeds now; I don't think you can even get down there"

Steph had a strange look on her face "You can get down there" she said mysteriously frowning deeply. "How do you know?" asked Wendy suspiciously. "I know because I saw someone down there a couple of weeks ago, I saw a man then he disappeared. At the time I thought I must be imagining things. It was getting dark but I thought I saw him at the bottom of the ramp by the side of the library. I shouted and he must have heard me.

I was a bit scared actually, but I knew Marie was inside, so I walked down the side of the building to the back of the disabled access ramp but when I got down there it was empty, there was no one there. I was baffled and a bit relieved if I'm honest, I thought it was going to be a homeless man or a drunk or something, but now I realise, that's where the entrance to the access alley is—he must have climbed over".

"Or walked straight through if it was Barry Thompson." Marie chipped in "Only one way to find out. Come on gang, let's go ghost hunting". She jumped up decisively.

They all clambered to catch up with Marie as she charged purposefully to the office "Right Steph you get scissors, we could do with shears, but scissors will have to do.

Rosie grab some string just in case and Wendy get some gloves out of the cleaners cupboard—I know they're only washing up gloves but needs must and those brambles will be sharp!" Matilda called out "What shall I do?" Marie stopped, trying to think of a job that made Matilda feel important without her needing to clamber over fences and brambles wearing pink marigolds armed with scissors and string.

"Matilda I think its important that someone Barry is familiar with stays in the staff room, just in case we scare him when we land in his alley and he wants to pop back into the library. He clearly feels a connection with you as he has shown himself to you three times." She kept her fingers crossed and wore her most sincere face while Matilda digested the implications of this important role, "Ok, I think you're right, he did choose me didn't he so if I stay here he has someone he feels safe with if you lot distress him. I've always thought I had a connection with the other side. Right well good luck girls" Matilda retreated purposefully into the staff room and immediately started looking for the biscuit tin.

The others collected outside in the cold afternoon, trying to look calm and purposeful and not attract attention from the people who live opposite—they already kept a keen eye on the library, the last thing the gang needed to do was explain what they were up to.

"Just in case anyone does see us and asks us what we're doing, we'll say we've had a report of a rat behind the library and we are going round to see if we can spot anything before calling environmental health—Ok?" Marie seemed cool and in charge, but her hands were a bit shaky as she rolled the rubber gloves on.

Quietly they all followed her up the side of the building to the back of the ramp, trying not to slip on the thin film of slush still on the ground. Even though it was not quite four o'clock, it was starting to get quite dark adding to the eerie atmosphere. Rosie suddenly whispered dramatically "I am late for tap dancing—Mrs Beaufort-Thistle will kill me!" Marie looked at her wide eyed and whispered just as dramatically "You cannot leave me here to do this! It's getting dark and I am only pretending to be brave!! Cant you call someone to take Billy and Lucy for you?"

Marie looked so spooked it pricked Rosie's conscience and she looked a bit sheepish. "Ok, I can ask my neighbour, Shiela. She picks her daughter Millie up and takes her to tap, but she doesn't normally stay and I do; I am supposed to be in the bloody show." She pulled out her mobile and started dialling, Marie looked relieved "I don't suppose one week will make any difference. Mrs Beauthingy-whatsit will forgive you one week—tell her it was a matter of life or death! Wendy—any chance you can pop and get us a torch while Rosie sorts out her childcare?"

Wendy gave Marie an indignant look but nodded, she wondered who put Marie in charge, standing there shouting instructions to everyone else. Then she thought about being at the front and having to climb over that old fence, the soggy brambles, the bugs and spiders not to mention the ghost and decided she would leave Marie to it.

She didn't have time to be a hero today, Mark was expecting her back at half past four and she didn't want to be late. He had promised to take her out tonight over to Kelly's to see her and the kids and pick up chips on the way.

Rosie finished her call and grinned mischievously at Marie, "I told her we had just found out about the death of a colleague and were sorting out some important things at work. I didn't mention we had found out from his ghost—thought that might be pushing it a bit. She was good as gold though, sounded like she was covering for a secret agent when she practiced what she had to say to Mrs Beaufort-Thistle for me.

Lucy is Millie's best friend too so they will have a nice time, although they do tend to leave Billy out a bit when they're together." Rosie was rambling and it looked like she was about to change her mind so Marie raised her eyebrows at her—that always did the trick, such a simple facial expression but it said; 'are you quite finished the ramblings of a lunatic now?' Rosie reacted to it immediately, calmed down and turned towards the library ramp.

Wendy arrived back with a torch "Don't ask me why we have this, I think the animal man left it the last time he came. He used it because he lost one of the glow worms and spent quite a long time in the reference section looking for it. Of course the kids thought it was hilarious, they kept shouting 'over there' 'over here' he was running round like a fool.

Eventually it turned up in the mop bucket, don't ask me how it got there. It still works, but, well here it is anyway." she handed a green and yellow snake shaped torch to Marie who raised her eyebrows again—wasted on Wendy; Marie's eyebrows didn't affect her at all.

They all followed Marie down the side of the library none of them eager to be at the front. They congregated in the area behind the top of the ramp trying not to look suspicious whilst lurking in the shadows.

"Damn it, do we have any ladders? I didn't realise how high the fence was. I can't reach the top." Marie whispered urgently "No ladders" stated Wendy bluntly. "Can't you climb on the outside of the ramp and edge along from the hand rail?" It sounded so perfectly easy, for a gymnast "Sure" mumbled Marie "Just call me spider woman. Anyone else want to give it a go?" Silence "Thought not".

She walked up the ramp to the top and dodged under the rail. If she leaned forwards and stretched her one leg out, she could reach the fence.

It would take a leap of faith—well just a leap actually cos she would need to launch herself onto the fence and grab the top to be able to use the ramp rail as leverage for her other leg. Perfect, good job it was her day off and she had jeans on; she wouldn't risk this in anything else. She called down to Steph "Steph, you're the tallest, can you reach up and chop any of these brambles off, you'd need to be a ghost not to get torn to shreds climbing over this fence—the thorns are lethal.

Hey maybe that's what happened, old Barry decided to pop behind the library for a jimmy riddle and got spiked on these bloody brambles, couldn't get back out and starved to death."

"Don't be ridiculous" exclaimed Wendy "what person in their right mind would go to all the trouble of climbing over all these brambles and rubbish to get to a bit of space untouched by anyone for years

just to do a wee? We have a perfectly adequate toilet in the library
and to be fair he could have done anything in that space behind the
ramp. No one could see there, he didn't need to climb over. But even
if he did, these walls are so thin he could have shouted to us and we
would have heard him. That space behind the ramp is dangerous,
I've always said so, ever since I caught those teenagers having sex
there two years ago, I could hear them in the office! I knew no good
would come of this empty space—just attracts trouble" Marie did
her eyebrows again, but it was too dark to see, she waited patiently
(ish) while Steph trimmed some of the brambles off which were
hanging over the fence with the craft scissors. She managed to clear
just enough so that Marie could get two hands on the top of the
fence. "Right here goes nothing" whispered Marie to herself, now
so consumed with the task of getting over the fence that she had
completely forgotten what was likely to be behind there.

She leapt forward and grabbed the fence, one leg resting against the
ramp rail and the other one stopping her body from crashing into a
world of pain from the brambles on one side of the fence and tarmac
on the other. She used the back leg to give her an extra push which
gave her just enough momentum to roll over the top of the fence
sideways.

Fortunately there were no witnesses to the most unladylike landing
ever, lucky too that the landing was broken by five or six years of ivy,
moss and leaves in various stages of decomposition which felt soft
and cold but slimy under the rubber gloves and jeans.

She sat still for a second or two internally checking for injuries. She
then called back (quietly) to the others that she was ok.

Turns out she was jumping the gun though because as soon as she put her torch on she could clearly see why Barry was pointing to this alley; his body or what was left of it, was lying immediately to the right of Marie like a best friend. Worse still the slimy thing she put her hand on as she righted herself when she first landed was not moss or decaying undergrowth, but Barry's head with the rotted flesh almost dripping off it. She screamed; the terrified sound piercing the silence created by the walls, vegetation and fence all around her.

Unfortunately due to the nature of her entrance to the alley, no one could get over to help or re assure her. She was on her own and scared rigid, literally tightening all her muscles to hold herself as rigid as she could without actually moving away from the body as there was nowhere to move to, just more prickles and bramble. The other's whisper shouted for her to calm down and breathe slowly. They wanted her to describe what she could see.

It took a few minutes for Marie to collect herself and allow her muscles to relax—not too much or she might wee in the fear of the moment, but enough that she could unclench her fists, eyes and mouth. None of this trying to relax was helped by the awful smell—it was like rancid and rotten meat and she knew from CSI on telly that it was the smell of decomposing Barry. She must have stirred the smell up when she landed.

She made herself breathe slowly with the torch off and reminded herself that she had gloves on so the rotting person wasn't actually on her hands, just the sensation of it. She shivered and swallowed to control the rising bile in her throat—enough bad smells around here already without her adding to them.

Ok, she told herself, pretend this is just a program on the telly, it's not a real dead person next to her. She breathed through her mouth to try and block out the smell. She held herself stiff and turned the torch on. For an instant she was filled with fear again, she expected immediate illumination but it was still dark. A heartbeat later she realised her eyes were still shut and allowed a nervous twitch of a smile to herself.

She prepared herself for another second before she opened her eyes and started to examine the scene. She decided to look all around without looking directly at Barry. She felt sure if she familiarised herself with her surroundings, knowing there was a dead body next to her, she might be less petrified when she actually looked at him.

The undergrowth where she had just landed was already flat and a bit of the fence behind her slightly to the right of where she had come over was broken and it wasn't fresh. It had a slightly darker colour than the bit she had just broken but wasn't as worn as the rest of the fence.

A big clump of the brambles were bent over and caught under Barry's body; in fact it looked as if Barry had somehow been thrown over the fence by the awkward way his body was laying.

"It's definitely Barry and he's definitely dead. He's not fresh either, he's almost black and the smell is shocking. The fence is a bit broken this side and the weeds are crushed and disturbed, but only around the body. Actually the fence looks as if it's been pushed in from your side. Ladies, I think he's been thrown over the fence—presumably after he was dead! Definitely foul play. I think one of you should phone the police right now and then work out how you are going to get me out of here." "Hang on" whisper shouted Rosie "see if you can spot any clues. Miss Marple always checks their pockets and looks to see if there is anything in their hands."

Marie took a breath to stop herself from shouting back and managed to keep her voice fairly quiet. "Maybe she does Rosie, but in those films the person who is dead is fresh and their flesh is not dripping off their bones! I am not going to look in his pockets and I can only see one hand."

She automatically looked at his hands as she spoke, her interest piqued by Rosie's suggestions at the same time as being appalled by the thought of touching the body "The other one seems to be twisted underneath him" all this through gritted teeth.

However, she noticed that the hand she could see was closed like a fist—the inquisitive half of her wanted to just reach over and poke the fingers apart just in case there was a clue in there; the other half of her was screaming at the first half to get out of the alley.

Just as she was considering whether to reach out, her phone lit up and made a doorbell noise—it made her jump so much she dropped the torch and squealed. She almost wet herself as well, only clenching her muscles in the nick of time. Bloody phone!

"What's wrong?" called Wendy urgently. Marie closed her eyes again "Apart from being trapped in a dark stinkingalleywith a dead person nothing Wend, my phone just went off, I must have a text".

Wendy made an interested noise that sounded like she thought the text message could be connected "You should check it" she whispered. Marie rolled her eyes in the darkness and used the phone light to find the torch.

She checked the message 'Hi baby, hope you are having a nice day off; can we have chips from the chippy tonight?' Merch—if only he knew. He would go mad if he found out about this crazy afternoon. "No connection, just Merch asking for chips. To be fair it was hardly likely to be Barry communicating via O2 to let me know what happened, was it?"

She was feeling a bit more confident now, the text message had somehow grounded her again and she was less scared and more intrigued. She picked a stick up and poked Barry's hand to see if she could open it without getting too close.

She still didn't look at his face. Nope, the handpoke just slimed the stick. She looked around for something more substantial to open the hand but there was nothing. It was no good she just couldn't leave without checking his hand.

She leaned over, supporting herself on the back fence to stop her falling entirely on top of Barry. In the back of her mind there was a tingle of fear, she knew the forensic people where going to be really cross when they found she had trampled the crime scene. She reasoned with herself that it was already trampled now anyway, so what harm could one more trample do?

She used the tip of her marigold to lift the first two fingers up and she could see something shiny in his fist, it was virtually impossible to keep the torch in her left hand that was against the fence and use her other hand to fish the shiny thing out of his hand. She put the torch in her mouth and used her fence hand to lean in and take out what looked like a little disc. She popped it in her coat pocket and sank back against the library wall, spitting out bits of foliage that had been stuck to the torch.

"Ok you guys, that's really enough now. Has someone phoned the police and have you worked out how to get me out of here? My bum is starting to feel really wet" Marie stage whispered. Steph replied in a normal voice which made Marie jump again because all the conversations since she had climbed the fence had been in whispers. "Yes, Rosie has gone to phone the police and Wendy has phoned Mark to come down with a ladder so you can climb back out". "Well I hope she told him to hurry up because this is the stuff of nightmares and I'm going to be in big trouble if the police arrive and I'm still round here"

Marie heard a deep breath sound from over the fence. "Well to be honest I think we are all going to be in big trouble whether you are still over there or not! The police don't like you messing with evidence—after all this could be a murder enquiry"

Steph sounded resigned but excited. Marie, however, sounded sarcastic "Steph, there's no 'could be' about it, it's definitely a murder enquiry. Suicides don't kill themselves then throw themselves over a fence!" Her voice turned to contemplative and reflective. "And I am positive he was thrown by the way he's landed. I cant tell what killed him though, not that I'm an expert, but I cant see a noose round his neck or a knife sticking out of him and its so dark I cant tell what might be blood, mud or congealed body slime" a gagging noise drifted over the fence "Oh Marie do you have to—you're making me feel sick, poor Barry."

Marie raised her eyebrows in mock surprise to herself "Oh you poor thing you! Did I upset your sensitivities? Don't worry about me feeling sick! And how about 'poor Marie'? It's disgusting over here, at least Barry cant smell himself or see the state of his body." Marie was getting a bit whiney now it was clearly time to get her out.

"You are uncouth Marie –I hope his poor ghost isn't listening to how disrespectful you're being" cautioned Steph in a quiet but resolute voice.

Before Marie had a chance to lecture Steph on how miserable it was for her, they heard a commotion and metal clanging. "Here we are, I have sorted out my old window cleaning ladders and am bringing them to the rescue." Mark said helpfully as he marched up to the rear of the library "Where do you want them?"

"Over here please Mark" called Marie politely. Mark looked at the fence questioningly. "My dear, what are you doing over there?" he enquired. Wendy chipped in hurriedly. "Don't worry about 'why' anything Mark. We need to get her out pronto.

The police are on their way and we all need to be safely back in the library before they arrive." Mark looked questioningly at Wendy but she clapped her hands together impatiently as if to hurry him along.

"Ok Marie, get ready. I am passing the ladder over the top of the fence now." Marie looked up behind her just as a loud scraping signalled the ladders appearing over the top of the fence. "Whoa, slowly start leaning them down or they'll go straight over the top of the alley."

She leaned up to catch the bottom rung of the ladder and slowly lowered them into the undergrowth. At least she wouldn't need anyone to foot the ladder; the alley was so narrow and tangled with undergrowth they couldn't go anywhere. What ensued next was worthy of a round of applause—anyone watching might have thought Marie was practicing pole dancing as she wrapped her body around the ladder sliding up and pulling on the rungs to extricate herself from the mess she was in.

She paused at the top of the ladders and turned to have one last look at Barry. She tried to see if from above the body you could make out any more clues, but she couldn't; it was too dark to see anything but a black body shaped blob.

A feeling of melancholy washed over her for the sadness of Barry's demise and the lack of caring for anyone to find out what had happened to him. Oh well, she had done her bit, they would leave it to the police to find justice now. At least they had found the body so hopefully Barry's ghost could rest in peace.

She scrambled over the fence, hanging by her marigolds from the top and finally dropping in a heap on the floor like a pile of rags.

She looked sorrowfully up at the others. Mark, Wendy and Steph stood staring uncertainly at her. "What??" she snapped from her crumpled position on the floor. "Well" said Steph gently "You are a bit. dirty and a bit dishevelled." Marie was flabbergasted at the injustice of it all, these people were unbelievable. "Really?" she asked, "I wonder why that is?" dramatic pause "Oh for goodness sake just help me up" She snapped, reaching her hands out to the trio. All three of them backed away. "You're kidding me? You don't want to touch me after you launched me into that bed of rotting undergrowth next to a decomposing corpse? What kind of friends are you?"

They had the grace to look a bit uncomfortable, but still didn't budge. Eventually she rolled herself over and got up, a bit shaky on her legs from all the drama. "Friends with a sense of smell?" Steph offered tentatively in a light hearted way. "Way too soon for jokes" Marie snarled menacingly.

Mark looked at Wendy as if the rest of the people there were deaf "Why is she wearing washing up gloves?" Wendy wafted her hands at him, "Because they were the only gloves we had" she said as if it were Mark that was daft. "Come on, we need to get Marie washed and find some clothes from the dressing up box before the police get here or they will be carting her off as a suspect."

Marie looked at Wendy mortified "Really? The dressing up box? How will that throw suspicion away from me? There are no normal clothes in there. Which do you think will be most innocent looking; the clown look or the nun do you think?"

Wendy jauntily looped her hand into Marie's arm, careful to keep all but her hand as far away as was polite and started off down the side of the library. Trying to appear oblivious to the smell and mess although not as close as she would normally be in an arm link.

"Don't be so sarcastic, we can check out the lost property box as well, I am sure we can fashion something that looks relatively normal" Wendy responded as positively as she could. "'Fashion' something? Was that fence a time line? Have I landed back in 1920? Wendy there is nothing in there that will make me look normal" Marie whined.

"No, probably not—its not a magic box after all—we'll just have to settle for what we can find wont we?" Wendy actually laughed this comment out.

"WE? You're all perfectly fine. It's me that will have to strip and wash in the freezing cold bloody toilet and wear clothes that are older than me. Then I'll have to explain to the police what I was doing rolling all over a crime scene. Ooh I am in such trouble, what were we thinking?" Marie wailed.

Wendy patted Marie's shoulder a bit tentatively and then looked at her hand with trepidation. "Don't worry honey, it will all be ok. We can just explain to the police about the ghost and that you innocently climbed over the fence not knowing that there was a body there. We have to be honest, but if we had called the police when we first saw the ghost, there is no way the police would have come out. They would more likely have sent a psychiatrist not a police officer if they'd taken any notice at all! I'm sure we'll be fine once we explain it all. Now calm down and get yourself inside before anyone smells, I mean sees you".

Wendy opened the library door and stepped back (quite far) for Marie to go in. She walked dejectedly through the library to the staff room where Matilda was waiting with tea already made. "Here you go dear. Oh, perhaps you had better wash and change before you sit down" she said blatant distaste all over her face. Marie looked thoroughly miserable.

"Here, I had this in my locker, one of the readers club gave it me for Christmas and I forgot to take it home." Steph passed Marie a Dove body wash set "you go and give yourself a good wash and put your clothes in this carrier bag, we can hide it in the cleaner's cupboard until the police have gone. I'll sort you some clothes out". Marie disconsolately sloped off into the toilet and the others breathed out again.

"Phew, that is some pong she's managed to get herself covered in, what is it?" Matilda asked quietly. "Barry" answered Steph and Rosie together.

Marie peeled her marigolds off and dropped them in the carrier bag. Then she took off her coat and gazed at it sadly—her favourite coat which would never be the same again. It was covered in mud, sludge and black stuff she didn't want to think about. She squashed it in the bag and quickly took off her jeans and jumper. Standing shivering in her sensible, non matching pants and bra she started lathering up the body wash under the hot tap on the plastic squeegee thing. Damn this freezing bloody toilet and its tiny sink and no plug. She used the squashy plastic white object to wash her legs arms and face and realised she had no moisturiser and no make up.

Great, now I look rough and old and nothing to disguise it she thought in a fed up voice. She was being a little hard on herself, she didn't look that bad, more rugged than rough but with the only mirror being made out of a shiny metal square, the overall effect dampened her spirits even more. Truth was she was feeling very sorry for herself and trying to decide who to blame. Then she remembered it was her idea to go investigating and that made her worse, she could feel tears prickling in her eyes when she thought about how she would explain this to the police and that while explaining it, she would look like a bag lady. She tried to gulp in air in an effort to clear the image of Barry lying in the undergrowth, but it wouldn't go. Every time she tried to focus on something else, like how much mud or slime was under her nails, the picture came back and with it a crushing horror, for being part of the scene in her head, and for Barry, for his part in the scene. His part was definitely worse.

Just as she could feel her throat constrict and pure panic take root in her stomach there was a knock at the toilet door and Rosie whispered "Are you decent?" She took a deep breath and forced control to suppress the terror. "Depends on what you call decent, I am standing in a freezing cold toilet in non matching bra and pants with no make up on and no matter how much I lather and wash I still smell like rotting meat" Marie responded thoroughly dejected. "Open the door then hun and you can try some of these clothes on" Rosie said encouragingly.

Marie opened the door and Rosie squeezed in. "Right; this jumper is quite nice. It was in the lost property box, it will be a bit big but not too bad". Marie eyed the jumper with disgust wondering which member of the readers club had taken any of their clothes off at the library and why.

The jumper was a lurid pink with an embroidered butterfly on the front—truly awful. She put it on, it looked like a sack. "There, lovely. Now I struggled for a bottom, so you have a choice of two; you can wear the clown trousers or the long black skirt from the nuns outfit. What do you think?"

Marie felt sick. "I think I might rather walk about in my pants." Rosie laughed "Don't be so melodramatic. Here try the skirt; with that jumper it will make you look a bit like a hippy. I think the trousers might make you look a bit odd because of the colours" She was clearly underestimating the possible colour situation. The trousers were balloon shaped with elastic at the ankles, bold striped creations in bright blue, yellow and green. "You think?" Marie said ironically. She took the skirt and put it on. "This is going to look great with my trainers" she said flatly.

They both looked down at the trainers which were obviously ruined. They were covered in soggy black stuff with ivy and brambles stuck to them. "Oh God Merch is going to kill me" Marie wailed as she started to crumble on to the floor. "Now now, don't be daft, take them off and wash your feet. I found these flip flops in your locker, they're the ones I got free in Cosmopolitan in the summer but were too big for me. Put your trainers in the bag and I'll take the lot to the laundrette. I'm sure they'll be good as new when you get them back."

Rosie had a forced smile on her face as she encouraged Marie back up to standing. They both knew none of the clothes would be suitable for wearing again no matter how many times they were washed.

"Flip flops in the snow? I wish I was dead" Marie moaned as she dropped her trainers and socks into the carrier bag and awkwardly lifted her feet, one at a time into the washbasin.

"Don't say that! I'm sure Barry would love to swap places with you. They're only clothes Marie, you can get home and get showered and changed before Merch gets back from work and he'll never know the difference." Rosie said firmly.

She could feel Marie building up to full blown hysterics and with the police coming, they needed to calmly spend a bit of time getting their story straight so she didn't have time to allow Marie a breakdown. "Come on now, your tea will be cold and Wendy's found some chocolate digestives to help with the shock." Rosie put her arm around Marie and started steering her back in to the staff room dumping the carrier bag full of ruined clothes into the cleaner's cupboard on the way.

The others were all sitting down tensely waiting, Matilda and Wendy on the chairs and Steph on the table. They had brought the office chair in for Marie to sit on and Mark had been sent home. They all went quiet when Marie and Rosie walked in. Wendy jumped up to guide Marie into the office chair and Matilda passed her a cup of tea. Steph took a biscuit out of the packet and gave it to Marie. "There" said Matilda "you look fine in those" Everyone looked at Matilda horrified. "What?" she said innocently "She looks ok to me." Marie seemed to shrink a bit further into the chair as she put the whole biscuit in her mouth.

"The police will be here any time now, so what are we going to say?" This from Rosie in a conspiratorial tone.

Wendy looked a bit surprised "We have to tell them what happened, that's what we'll do, they'll understand. We had to have a look ourselves before we called them or they would have accused us of wasting police time. We couldn't just phone up the police and say 'Officer, we have a ghost in the library staff room that is pointing to the back wall. Can you send some officers to climb over the fence and investigate behind the library for us?' they'd think we're a bunch of mad women."

Rosie sighed and said "As opposed to saying 'officer, we have found a dead body hidden behind the library—oh how did we find it, you say? Why a ghost told us!'

We can't tell them a ghost pointed to the wall then floated through and that's why we went round there. They will still think we are a bunch of mad women. No we have to come up with a credible reason for why we went to look behind the library. Now we have to consider—what could that be?"

Matilda put her hand up, then back down "I was going to say we could tell them we were playing a ball game down the side of the building and the ball went over, but then I realised they probably wouldn't believe us because we're not really dressed for ball games." Marie looked at Matilda as if she was more bonkers than usual "Not dressed for ball games? Its mid winter, melted snow is everywhere and we range in age from forty's to seventy's. Most of you and me now, are in dresses and I am wearing flip flops! If we can't tell them the truth we have to come up with something simple.

If we create some complicated story one or more of us will forget some of the details and we will all end up in the slammer for perverting the course of justice!" Everyone went quiet thinking about the enormity of what had happened and how much trouble they might be in.

They were wracking their brains to come up with a reasonable story about why they would have gone behind the library when the staff door opened. Rosie squealed and they all jumped. Standing in the doorway was Sergeant Roberts, the local police who often popped into the library if he was in the area. He was a young man, but he strongly believed that it was seeing a police officer on the street that was the most important component of a happy and crime free community. He made sure that even though he had made Sergeant, he still walked the beat whenever he could, even including a visit every now and again to the local shops and schools.

All the ladies expelled a loud sigh together; Rosie squeaked "How did you get in the library officer?" Sergeant Roberts looked a bit puzzled "Through the door, of course, it was unlocked." They all looked at each other believing one of the other's should have locked it. Wendy said "Never mind that, thank goodness its you Daniel, we're in a terrible mess." He went to speak but Wendy put her hand up to stop him "No, let me speak first. This place will be crawling with police officers any minute now and they will be bringing forensics and everything." Sergeant Roberts looked a bit cautious "So you did call the police then? I was up at West Heath Juniors and I got a message from the station saying a hysterical woman had phoned to say somebody was stuck behind the library they asked me to pop in—but there's no one else coming, just me. So who's stuck and have you called the fire brigade?"

They all looked at Rosie, she looked offended. "I was not hysterical, and I clearly said there is a body in thealleybehind the library, your operator couldn't have been listening properly" she said defensively. Sergeant Roberts did a comic double take at Rosie, "Are you telling me there is a real live body behind the library?" he was smiling at her as if she was small child. Matilda said "Don't be silly Daniel; you can't have a real live body. Bodies are dead or we wouldn't have called it a body we would have called it a person"

His smile faded "So you are actually saying there is a dead body behind the library? It's not a joke?" Wendy had her very serious face on.

", we would not dream of wasting police time in these days of cuts and austerity; that would be a crime." she smiled at her own phrasing "There is the murdered body of Barry Thompson ex supply pool staff from Northfield library lying behind the library."

Sergeant Roberts went a bit pale as he realised they weren't joking "How do you know? How did you find it?" he asked. Most of the ladies stayed silent desperately hoping that one of the others would come up with a credible explanation, but before anyone could have a go, Matilda piped up "His ghost came into the staff room here and showed us where it was". If a silence could be described as dramatic, there was a dramatic silence.

Sergeant Roberts was conflicted; on one hand he had never had a murder on his patch or even an unidentified body. You couldn't really count the body of Eric Bernard which was found balanced on his bicycle outside the post office one Monday in 2009.

The only reason that one might not count was that he had died of natural causes; it just stuck in his mind because the body balanced on the bike for nine hours before anyone reported anything suspicious. The post office staff just thought he had dropped off to sleep (he was a notorious drinker) and no one wanted to wake him due to his reputation for vomiting as soon as he woke up from drink induced stupor.

On the other hand he was imagining his prospects of becoming Inspector floating off into the distance when he tried to radio in a report about a body which had been found by a bunch of eccentric women who said a ghost had told them where it was.

"How about a nice cup of tea while we have a think about this then?" he said in his best police officer voice. The ladies look astounded "What? Tea? There is a murdered man rotting away out there and you, a police officer suggest we calmly sit here warming the pot! You need to get your buddies here quick sharp young man and get this poor mans body out and his murderer behind bars as soon as possible"

Wendy barked out ferociously.

Sergeant Roberts put his hands out pleadingly "Now steady the bus there Wend, lets calm ourselves down. You have to admit it all sounds a bit far fetched. A ghost told you there was a body behind the library? Did he tell you who it was?" he asked, looking from Wendy to Steph "We didn't say he told us where the body was actually, he didn't speak, he just pointed to the library back wall and walked though it.

He sort of demonstrated where it was. And we've already told you who he is, he's Barry Thompson and we know that because it's his ghost that showed us where the body was" Steph explained calmly.

Sergeant Roberts was definitely starting to wish he'd stayed at the school "Well, before I radio anything in I will have to see the body with my own eyes, so who can show me where it is?" The ladies all looked at Marie; Sergeant Roberts looked at her too, he though she looked like she was a bit simple, he knelt down to look directly into her face "Do you know whereabouts the body is love? Can you show me?" he said gently. Marie looked up at him and went bright red "Don't talk to me like I'm an idiot! And you can all bugger off, I'm not going back behind there, you can arrest me here and now" She dramatically put her wrists up for imaginary handcuffs, "course you'll need to be quick before the fashion police arrive and cart me off".

Sergeant Roberts stumbled backwards and nearly fell flat on his back just catching himself on the coffee table, "Marie?? What the hell happened to you? You look terrible. I had no idea it was you" Marie smirked at him "Cheers officer I feel so much better now. Where to start? I have been cosying up with a rotting corpse in a stinking filthyalleyafter a tip from a ghost! So a bit of sympathy wouldn't go amiss"

He looked at her clothes and finished off staring at the flip flops "You've been out dressed like that?" He looked unconvinced.

"Of course not! My own clothes were ruined by . . ." she didn't finish her sentence; she had suddenly remembered the shiny disc she had taken out of Barry's hand. Everyone looked expectedly at her, she jumped up and said "excuse me" and hurried out of the room towards the toilet. The room was quiet for a couple of seconds. Matilda coughed "She has had a bit of a shock and that always upsets my stomach too"

A couple of minutes later, Marie rushed back into the room with what looked like a piece of toilet roll between her fingers; everyone gaped in disgust.

"This was in his hand" she carefully put the unidentifiable thing stuck to toilet paper on the table and everyone gathered round. "What is it?" asked Rosie. "I don't know, but he was holding it in his hand so I figured it could be a clue"

Sergeant Roberts stood back up straight his face a picture of horror "You took this from the body? From the victim? You have tampered with evidence—what were you thinking??" His voice was getting louder "You could be charged with perverting the course of justice or interfering with evidence! You will have contaminated the area, the victim and you may well have destroyed any chance of us finding clues as to who the murderer is, if indeed there has been a murder!"

He was red in the face by the end of his righteous tirade. Rosie looked petrified but the others hadn't even stopped examining the artefact

"Oh stop being so stuffy, come and help us identify what it is, and if you like I can put it back after" Marie said ending in a conspiratorial voice.

Sergeant Roberts was flabbergasted, what were these women on? Had he slipped at the school and banged his head and woken up in an Agatha Christie novel? Could any of this be true? He stood still for a moment and pinched himself—yep he felt it, but surely he couldn't be awake, this couldn't be real? He could feel a dull ache starting to throb in his temple.

Matilda noticed he was standing very still. His eyes had glazed over and his face had started twitching on one side. "You know, I think your idea about a cup of tea was a good one, I'll put the kettle on" she gently guided Sergeant Roberts to the office chair, he went very meekly.

"It looks like a coin" said Steph. She leaned closer and used a pencil to hook a bit of the toilet paper to try and wipe some gunk off the disc. "Bloody hell, it's a trolley coin" said Rosie "a Tesco trolley coin; for the shopping trolley." "We know what a trolley coin is Rosie" Marie snapped. She was a bit put out that Rosie had identified the object before she had worked out what it was. She felt a bit protective about the whole body and shiny coin thing; after all it was her that had found them both.

"Oh great" said Matilda coming back in with a tray of mugs full of tea "I've lost mine and I never have a pound in my purse when I go shopping." She gently laid the tray on the table. "You can't have it, Matilda, it's a clue, its evidence—it could be the key couldn't it Sergeant Roberts?" asked Wendy.

He looked a bit bewildered "Well probably not now you've removed it from the scene and wiped it clean to be honest.

Anyway, don't talk to me for a minute, I am trying to work out what the hell I am going to do and I cant think while you lot are babbling on." Wendy looked offended. "Sergeant Roberts, there is no need to be rude. We are simply concerned citizens trying to help solve a crime in times of reduced police services" she said in her best indignant voice. He looked up at her threateningly over his mug of tea" We don't even know if a crime has been committed yet! It's dark and Marie could have been mistaken, and concerned citizens don't go around reporting ghosts and stealing evidence." He sounded exasperated even to himself, but he felt like he was in a dream or more accurately a comic nightmare.

He couldn't even bring himself to go and look to see if there was a body behind the library because he didn't know what he would put in his report if there was. He did know however, that he couldn't put the truth down—no one would believe it. He was living it and he didn't even believe it. He felt a momentous crushing feeling, like realising your career was over and there was nothing you could do to stop it.

He had mishandled this whole incident and if his superiors ever found out, his P45 would be in the post.

A sinking feeling had him huddling round his tea. No need to panic, he told himself, he just needed a few minutes to collect his thoughts, and if there was a body it wasn't going anywhere.

The ladies however, were perfectly collected and couldn't believe Sergeant Roberts was so reluctant to act. "You have to call it in; we have the body of a dead person behind the library!

We have to open tomorrow and its family reading group, we can't just leave him there. Regardless of your reservations, it's definitely a murder. I assure you there is no way someone would make all the effort to climb over that fence to die of natural causes at such an awkward angle. We need forensics and crime scene people and big lights, what's wrong with you?" Marie was starting to get hysterical.

Sergeant Roberts sat listening and trying to make some sense in his head. He got up and put his mug on the table ready to take some decisive action "Right first things first; you are going to show me where the body is and second we are all going to keep what has happened so far entirely secret between us until I work out how I can report this if there is actually a body."

Marie looked exasperated at his doubt of her story but just as she was about to launch into Sergeant Roberts the staff room door flew open again—this time only Sergeant Roberts squealed.

"Hi ladies, is mom here?" Ashlea, Marie's daughter thought of the library as her second home, her mom had worked there since she was eighteen months old and she had grown up with the library ladies, consequently she breezed in and out of the library when ever she wanted. Clearly they had still not locked the door.

Steph tried to discretely point at Marie, Ashlea looked down; her face took on an expression as if she was looking at pig innards close up "Oh my God what happened to you? Have you been attacked? Are you ill?"

She franticly looked from person to person "What is wrong with her? Why is she dressed like this?" Marie stood up and grabbed Ashlea's shoulders.

"Calm down Ash, I'm ok—well ok for someone who has had the day I have. Look, we met here to see a ghost that Matilda told us about. He pointed to the back wall and floated through it. Steph recognised who he was—Barry from Northfield library and then I climbed over the fence behind the disabled access ramp and landed next to his dead body. After scrambling about a bit, Wendy's Mark came down and brought a ladder so I could climb back over and because I was covered in body gloop and moss and mud. I stank, so I had to wash and take my clothes off and the only other clothes were in the dressing up box and lost property box so that's what I'm wearing." she smiled, the story finished a little triumphantly. Ashlea didn't move but said quietly "What's wrong with her? Why is she being barmy?" Marie shook her a little bit "Hello, I can hear you and speak. It's true I tell you, why don't you believe me?"

Ashlea wrinkled her nose up "Firstly because it all sounds ridiculous, like one of your daft Poirot books. And secondly because it sounds ridiculous! You don't believe in ghosts and neither do I. I cant believe you have been body hunting however I do believe those clothes came from the lost property box and dressing up box and I think you should return them there as a matter of urgency!" She looked at Sergeant Roberts "Have you come to Section my mom?" she whispered

"Ashlea! You need a doctor to Section someone and I am not insane! Come with us outside and you'll soon see its true, you too Sergeant Sceptical come on."

Marie grabbed Ashlea's hand and pulled the staff room door open and held it open ushering the others through it.

Sergeant Roberts grumbled "Well keeping it secret between us didn't last very long did it?" He was wasting his voice and knew it; the ladies just ignored him and started filing out of the room. Marie used dramatic eye rolling to try and hurry people up and then followed them all down the now completely dark library. "Steph, put the lights on will you? And the outside ones and pass the torch back over here." Marie was stretching over the counter and trying not to knock the books piled up there over. "No, don't put the outside lights on, I don't want to draw any attention to us." Sergeant Roberts panicked "We already have one more person than I wanted in on this farce" He looked pointedly at Ashlea, she looked defiantly back at him "Me? Why shouldn't I be here—the door was open wasn't it. If you don't want people to come in you should lock it! You're lucky it wasn't one of the borrowers. Besides, you don't actually believe this story do you? I thought policemen were supposed to be sensible."

He looked a bit uncomfortable and squinted his eyes at her, but didn't seem to be able to bring himself to respond so after a minute Ashlea just tutted and went to find her mom.

Outside the library it was really dark now, amazingly it was only quarter to five but it felt to the ladies like they had been there forever. It was very cold now too.

Rosie thought that was probably a good thing because she knew cold preserved bodies, so hopefully Barry won't have decomposed any further since Marie found him. She was starting to worry about getting home. If they had to wait to give their story to goodness knows how many other people and maybe have their clothes bagged or whatever, it could be hours before she got home and Mick would be starving and wondering where she and the kids were.

Steph was also getting a bit jaded. She had enjoyed the whole see the ghost find the body episode, but she was tired now and really wanted to sit down for a bit and have a nice glass of wine, preferably in someone else's house so that her girls and Nigel didn't have 100% call on all her time and attention. Oh to have a bit of peace and quiet, what was she thinking when she thought this whole ghost thing would be fun? It was just tragic, some poor lonely man had somehow got himself killed and he had to haunt strangers or no one would ever have known. Her shoulders drooped at the sadness of it.

Wendy was glad she had had the presence of mind to ask Mark to leave the ladder and his torch, which was much more powerful than the animal mans one. Sergeant Roberts would see the body and call in the troops and she and the other ladies would be heralded as local heroes for finding this poor soul's body. She just hoped the whole process would speed up a bit now, Mark had said he was getting ready when he left here and she didn't want to be messing about down at the library for hours. She was only paid till half past four.

Matilda stayed inside the library again, no one had said anything, but she knew it was her responsibility to stay in the staff room in case Barry's ghost got upset by all the goings on and came back into the library. She sat down on the chair by the table and helped herself to a chocolate digestive. After munching it quickly, she leaned her head on the back wall and put her feet up on the office chair. She closed her eyes and assured herself that she was just resting her eyes and if Barry came back she would know. Then she drifted off to sleep.

Marie and Ashlea reached the fence and Ashlea got a whiff of a smell she recognised only too well. She was a housing officer and part of her job was dealing with abandoned properties anti social behaviour and so on. About six weeks earlier she had been called out to a flat by a woman complaining that brown smelly fluid was dripping through her light fitting. Ashlea had gone to speak to the woman and witnessed the foul smelling fluid in the bowl under the light. No one had managed to get hold of Mr White who lived upstairs so Ashlea had arranged for the works carpenter to meet her to break in just in case the property had been abandoned and something was leaking.

She hadn't been that lucky, what she found when they got in was Mr Whites carer dead in the living room. It was his bodily fluid's that had seeped through the floor to the flat below over the last couple of weeks since he had been lying there. According to the post mortem, he had died of a heart attack.

She had spent twenty minutes calling the relevant authorities and following the appropriate processes, only to walk into the bedroom and find Mr White in bed; he was also dead. She found out later that he had been dead nearly two weeks as well, he died because he hadn't had his medication because the carer had died and he was bed bound so couldn't get them himself. It still made her shiver; horror movie stuff.

That was the smell she could smell now. It slowly dawned on her that perhaps her mom and her dippy friends were not bonkers after all—that smell was definitely a decomposing body. She looked at Sergeant Roberts. She could see the same thought process crossing his features, and he had obviously smelt it too.

Sergeant Roberts stepped forward lifting himself to his full height all sensible and taking control "Right, stand back you lot, I'll have a look over the fence without actually climbing over and doing any more damage and see if I can see anything." He picked up the ladder which was leaning against the ramp and placed it against the fence where the bramble had been cut away earlier. He climbed the ladder praying it was an animal, but knowing in his heart that it wasn't. He got to the top of the ladder and leaned against the fence to turn the torch on.

The darkness suddenly illuminated he immediately saw Barry's twisted body; he unconsciously made a low moaning noise and felt a tickle in his stomach that felt a bit too much like a bowel movement threatening.

"Right everyone back inside." He barked as he started climbing down the ladder backwards and shouting instructions as he reached each rung.

"Quickly and quietly get yourselves back into the staff room and I will follow you in with this ladder and lock the door behind us so no one else can bumble into this rather sensitive situation" he had snapped so swiftly into law and order mode that everyone automatically did what he said and clambered to get back into the library.

Once they were safely inside and Matilda had been woken up to join the discussions, he found himself coming to from his nightmare afternoon. The reality of the dead body and his need to deal with it meant the noise of the library ladies didn't bother him anymore and suddenly he had a moment of complete clarity.

"Right you lot sit down" he commanded—so loud that the ladies stumbled about trying to get a seat; the problem was there are only three chairs (even with the office chair) and one person can fit on the table. It was like musical chairs once the music stops; Ashlea quickly sat on Marie's lap and Matilda did the same with Rosie "Ooh" a muffled voice called from underneath Matilda, "Perhaps I should sit on you" Rosie suggested from underneath Matilda.

Matilda looked round and down at the tiny Rosie underneath her "You're probably right dear. Let's swap places." They all looked at Sergeant Robert expectantly.

"I've got it!" Sergeant Roberts declared in a eureka way and then he stood awaiting everyone's attention; he deliberately left a dramatic pause for his brilliance to sink in and be appreciated.

The problem with any gap in conversation with the library ladies around is there is always someone ready to fill it "Oh how clever" said Matilda clapping joyfully

"No wonder they made you a sergeant so young. What gave it away? Don't keep us in suspense—who did it?" They all looked at Sergeant Roberts eagerly and Wendy said "Hip hip hurray, hip hip . . ." and they all clapped and said "Hurray!"

Sergeant Roberts looked like he was going to burst "Don't be so ridiculous" he blustered "I haven't worked out what's happened, just how to report it. How could I possibly have solved the crime already?"

Matilda looked a bit crestfallen "Well there is the clue" she mumbled. "The CLUE??" he squealed "It's a bloody trolley coin not the name and address of the murderer. Even Sherlock Holmes couldn't solve a case that quickly from a trolley coin" his voice got louder with each word, absolutely exasperated by the women.

Marie looked as if she was about to disagree with his comment about Sherlock Holmes, being a big fan, but she noticed that the his neck had gone a purple colour and he looked about to explode, so she decided to keep her opinion on the matter to herself for the time being.

"No I have decided how we can report this crime without you lot being carted off to the funny farm and me being demoted back to traffic. Here's how it goes; you were all sitting here having a break when you heard a squealing noise behind the library. Ok so far?" They all nodded. "You decide it was probably a cat or dog trapped in the alley and so launch a rescue party."

Matilda put her hand up and the sergeant raised his eyebrows to signify she could speak. "It could have been fox" she said helpfully "It might not be a cat or a dog, fox's squeal too."

The library ladies and Ashlea were used to Matilda getting caught up in something and going off at an irrelevant tangent, but Sergeant Roberts looked puzzled as if she were trying to catch him out.

He continued slowly as if he thought they were trying to test him. "Ok, you don't know what the animal is, it's just an animal noise and you all go off round the back of the library to find out if you can help it out, whatever it is. But when Marie tries to lean over the fence, she falls and lands next to the body. The reason she has the token is that before she noticed the body she saw the shiny disc and thought it was money so put it in her pocket and didn't connect it to the body until you all came back in here. Is everyone clear? Can you all remember that?" the ladies all nodded silently. "Good. Start writing down your statements but miss the ghost bit out and the deliberately checking the body for clues and add in the animal noise. I am going to radio this in now." He sighed with relief and walked out into the main library. They could hear him using his official police voice to report the discovery of a body behind the library.

Wendy passed everyone a note book "Not you Ash, because you weren't here for the discovery of the body. You go and make us all a nice cuppa, we've had quite a day" Ashlea reluctantly made her way to the kitchen and put the kettle on. They all quietly started carefully writing down the events of the day and wishing it was all over.

The next two hour's were bedlam. The library and the alley were full of police officers and people in white suits. Lights were set up outside, huge white plastic sheets were draped everywhere and anything not covered in a sheet was cordoned off with red stripy tape. People were even on the roof taking photographs.

A couple of the officers came to speak to the ladies when they first arrived and their statements were collected, but after that they mostly left them alone and they stayed out of the way in the staff room, with the exception of when they run out of milk.

Ashlea volunteered to go the Tesco store on the opposite side of the road to the library and came back glowing and full of how exciting it looked from the outside and how many people had stopped her to ask what was going on.

She was flustered and excited "I didn't tell them anything, I said 'unfortunately evidence appears to suggest that a crime has been committed and I'm not at liberty to discuss the details with anyone outside the investigating team.' But they were really nosy—trying to work it out for themselves. Then just as I was coming back over here, they lifted the stretcher with the body in a body bag on over the fence and there was a big 'ahh' from the crowd. It's so exciting I can't bear it, my phone hasn't stopped since the police vans arrived and a lovely police constable out the front has asked me for my number! This is the best day ever!" she scooted into the kitchen to put the milk in the fridge and then flamboyantly flopped in one of the chairs.

Finally at seven o'clock the library ladies were told they could go home. They collected their coats and gave the library keys to the police.

The police officers promised to wash up any cups they used, post the keys back into the library and close the shutter. Tired and weary the library ladies made their way to their cars and Ashlea waved them all off, still full of youthful energy (she only lived five minutes from the library and had walked down).

Gerald was waiting outside the library to take Matilda home. He had already been once at five o'clock when she was due to finish, but had been sent away by the police. Matilda filled him in on the journey home and Gerald wondered how such an innocent looking woman could get caught up in so many real life adventures. For once he could see that the whole thing had drained her, she looked tired and pale. He said "Well I don't know about you, but with all this excitement I think we deserve a treat. Let's have our dinner at the Harvester in Bromsgrove. It's too late to cook now anyway."

Matilda beamed, absolutely delighted. She felt a happy glow which originated in her chest from Gerald being so understanding and nice and settled in her stomach knowing she was going to have a lovely dinner cooked by someone else. She settled back into her seat, folded her hands across her lap and closed her eyes for the journey.

Wendy arrived home to a house full of people, Mark announced to the room "I called the girls when I got back from the library and they all wanted to come and hear your exciting tale. We have chips and fish keeping warm in the oven, bread and butter on the side and a nice glass of wine to help calm your nerves." Wendy was overjoyed, her youngest grandson came careening into her legs and she lifted him to kiss his warm smooth little face and cuddle him.

They all looked at her expectantly as she took her coat off with one hand while expertly keeping hold of Ben with the other. She sat down on the settee and sighed dramatically ready to start the story for her avid audience and held her hand out for her wine.

Steph drove home in a dream. She couldn't believe what had happened in this day. This time yesterday she was imagining all sorts of endings to Matilda's ghost story, but the reality was so much more bizarre, she couldn't quite comprehend the way the actual events had unfolded. She had five texts on her phone when she finally got out of the library; three from Nigel (one of which she had replied to, just telling him she was going to be late and not why) and two from Gilly asking what was for dinner.

She pulled up outside her house where it appeared all the lights in the house were on, burning the free electric no doubt. She felt weary and unusually for Steph, irritable. She let herself into the hallway and was surrounded by a wall of noise; the girls were talking, well, shouting to each other over the noise of their music and from their own rooms and Nigel was in the lounge watching the news. Between them they were creating such a din that no one had heard her come in. "SHUT UUUP" she screamed in a very very high pitched loud voice. Within a couple of seconds, the music went off and three heads appeared at the top of the stairs.

Even Nigel came out into the hall and taking in Steph's unusual appearance he said gently "What's up love?" He thought Steph looked like she might burst into tears at any moment and she shook as she launched into her explanation.

"We found a dead body behind the library today—that's why I'm so late, in case any of you bothered to wonder" she said rather stroppily.

Immediately everyone jumped into action, Nigel put his arm around Steph and started to help her with her coat "Bella make the tea for your mom, Genie cheese on toast for everyone please."

The two girls who had been given tasks looked like they might say something, but the look in their dad's eyes and the way their mom was leaning on him kept their mouth's shut for a change. "Come and sit down and tell us all about it" Nigel said as he tenderly steered her to the settee.

Steph felt happier immediately. She was being spoilt and was the centre of attention—this never happened to her. She was always the one doing the placating and spoiling and she never had the most interesting stories—certainly not interesting enough to hold Nigel and all the girls' attention. She settled down contentedly to make the most of it.

Rosie was a bit worried about picking the children up; she had thought she would be back by about four thirty but now it was more than two hours after that. She had text Sheila to say that there was a drama at the library and she would be late and Sheila had text back that she was feeding the kids and they were watching a film so not to worry.

Mick was still at work; he was waiting by a freezing cold bridge in Coventry while the police were trying to talk a potential suicide down so he wasn't in a position to even know she was late or why.

He had text Rosie earlier to say he didn't know when he would be home and that he had eaten chips, so there was no need to save him dinner. She was disappointed, she had so much to tell him about her day and now there was no chance of having a grown up to talk to tonight.

She pulled up outside Shiela's and turned the engine off. She just sat for a minute letting herself relax and trying to compose herself so she didn't burst into tears when Sheila opened the door. She needed to prepare for the evening ahead with two small but boisterous and opinionated children. Well at least she wouldn't have to cook; she might just bake a cake or possibly just have a nice large glass of port and some toast.

She sighed dramatically and got out of the car climbing heavily up the steps to Sheila's house. The door swung open before she reached for the bell making her jump for about the hundredth time that day. Sheila was animated as she grabbed Rosie and pulled her inside "Oh my friend Bob just called me to tell me about all the drama at the library. I couldn't believe it—I am looking after the children of one of the ladies involved! I have been bursting to find out what's been happening. I hope you don't mind, I've made you a sandwich and poured you a glass of wine. The kids are happy for another hour or so and Bill's out at the club so how about it? Stay with me for a bit and tell me all about it, nothing exciting ever happens to anyone I know."

She eagerly tugged at Rosie's arm. Rosie smiled back and happily co operated as Sheila started taking her coat off for her and guided her into the lovely warm kitchen.

She glanced into the living room as she went past and the children were all transfixed by Aladdin. She glided into a comfy chair and took the sandwich and glass of wine as they were offered.

Mmm, she thought as she bit into the cheese salad sandwich, today is turning out to be quite a day—she looked up to see Sheila waiting expectantly, she swallowed her lump of sandwich and launched into her story.

Marie got home to find Merch waiting in the living room. "What we having for tea then, did you get chips?" he called without even looking up. "I'm starving." Marie could feel tears prickle and her sorry for herself temper start to rise up.

"Oh hi love, how was your day? Oh not bad really, saw a ghost, climbed over a fence and landed in rotting vegetation next to a decomposing body. Then spent hours working out a story to cover what had really happened and trying to prove I wasn't a nutter wearing clothes no one would dream of putting together from the lost property box. Then being interviewed by police who seemed to think I might be a suspect—how was your day??!" Marie's voice had got steadily louder as the rant had gone on and half way through Merch had come to stand in the entrance hall. He looked a bit scared, especially as he took in the clothes she had on.

He hesitated for a second once she had finished. "Sounds to me like someone needs a nice long soak in a bubble bath." He ventured in an overly theatrical voice.

"I'll make you a lovely cup of tea and order a Chinese take away for us. Then you can come and tell me all about it."

He moved up to her and put his arms round her, and gently started guiding her up the stairs towards the bathroom. "Off you go Mave, have a nice soak and get into your pyjamas and by the time you've relaxed the food will be here. I'll bring your tea up, sounds like you've got quite a story to tell". Marie's body sagged and she immediately started to relax, a bath would be lovely. She could still smell that rotten stink and she definitely felt a bit sore from where she crashed against the fence and onto the floor of the alley. She hadn't really had time to think about her aches and pains in the crazy afternoon since they saw the ghost.

She wondered what Merch would make of it all and if she was supposed to tell him the animal noise version or the real ghost version. Oh well, she would tell him the real version and bugger it; he was hardly likely to see any policemen to contradict the official story.

CHAPTER THREE

The next day dawned bright and crisp, with the big yellow sun glowing low in the sky and reflecting off the last little piles of snow still left over from the weekend's snowfall. The roads and paths were much clearer today so the cars were driving normally and people cautiously venturing out in their colourful hats and scarves and sensible winter boots.

The trees looked like works of art, all elegant and beautiful and as Rosie gazed out of the window, she absorbed the splendour and reflected on the day before. With a good nights sleep behind her she felt calm and reflective. She considered what might have happened to poor Barry Thompson. What had killed him? Marie had to be right, it couldn't have been natural circumstances, it had to be murder. But even though she listened as carefully as she could to what the police were saying yesterday, she still had no clue of what could have killed him. Even more perplexing, who on earth would want to kill quiet unassuming Barry?

Ah well, time for reflection was clearly over, she could hear Lucy and Billy playing in Lucy's bedroom, so it was time for action. Breakfast, wash, dress and off to school, then down to the library to get the books ready for the family reading group and see if anything else had been turned up after they left last night.

Wendy lay in bed listening to Mark whistling while he made tea; oh she was happy that she was off work today. She loved being at home; she had always been a home body and didn't really like working, although if she had to work, she did actually think that her job at the library was the perfect one. Flexibility to a degree, not too much pressure and in her own way, she loved the other library ladies—despite their obvious flaws.

Remembering the drama of the day before she had a flicker of regret that she wasn't in work that almost took over her pleasure that she wasn't.

She just thought it would be nice to talk over the events of yesterday and see if anyone had found anything else out. Oh well, not to worry, she was in on Friday so her curiosity would just have to wait, she settled back into her pillow to wait for her cup of tea to be delivered.

Matilda didn't feel very well when she woke up, her stomach was growling and she had a feeling that something in the meal the night before didn't agree with her delicate constitution.

Gerald was already up and was no doubt half way to the newsagents to pick up his daily paper. He will have left a pot of tea downstairs with a cosy over the pot knowing Matilda always woke up at the same time.

She crept stiffly out of bed, pulled on her warmest dressing gown and made her way to the toilet. Sitting there she thought back to the day before. Who could have guessed how it would turn out; even she couldn't have made this story up. She felt real sorrow for Barry, the poor victim that no one had even missed. It reminded her of the stories you hear about old people dying in their own home alone and not being discovered for weeks—the older you get the more those stories scared you.

Matilda realised she was going to be on the toilet for a while so she leaned across to get her book. She might as well relax while she was here; she only wished she had dashed down for a cup of tea to bring up before she had sat down. Never mind, it would stay hot and she decided not to go to the library today. She really needed a rest she felt weary and old.

She would do nothing today, just potter about, read her book and perhaps do a bit of dusting. She opened her book at the bookmark and started reading

Steph had overslept; that hadn't happened since before she had the girls. She had just got so carried away with the story and the family last night that they had accidentally drunk two bottles of wine and washed the cheese on toast down with trifle.

She didn't come to bed till nearly two in the morning and she was usually tucked up by eleven o'clock. She smiled to herself, she had really enjoyed the evening; it had felt like a really lovely family evening, no one argued, no one was mean to anyone else and no one sodded off to the pub.

Unfortunately she now had to face the day with a thick head and no time for breakfast so she rolled out of bed and plodded to the bathroom.

She felt a bit better once she had showered and put her hair up and she headed out the door at exactly the same time as always pocketing a cereal bar as she left. It would be a couple of hours before she noticed she had odd shoes on.

Marie woke to a radio DJ speaking irritatingly loud from the clock radio about something highly unlikely to be interesting to anyone but him. She leaned up to press snooze then remembered she had already pressed it once which meant it was time to get up. She dopily threw the quilt off and stumbled out of bed and into the back bedroom to get her towels off the radiator and head into the shower. She couldn't manage a coherent thought until she was standing under the shower.

She could hear Merch making tea downstairs and remembered the lovely evening they had once she was clean and calm. She didn't think he believed the ghost bit of the story, but it didn't matter, they had a nice time talking about every detail and it made a change from talking about what car Merch was looking at on Ebay or how his latest car or motorbike project was going. Now, the cold light of day made yesterdays antics less like a jolly adventure with the girls and more like a tragic tale of modern society. She climbed out of the shower, wrapped the warm towels around her and wandered out to start her day.

The ladies all pulled up outside the library at exactly eight thirty, every one of them thinking they were going to be late. Amid the hustle and bustle of the getting out of cars, clutching lunches and books to return they managed to raise the shutter and disarm the alarm without mishap.

They walked slowly through the library, their mood subdued. They all felt something different; perhaps the library would never feel the same again. Only twenty four hours before none of them believed in ghosts, none had seen a dead body and the most exciting thing that had happened to any of them was when they had all gone on a day trip to the Coronation Street set. They were having a lovely day when Rosie spotted Vera Duckworth just as she called out 'Rosie, come here'—our Rosie thought she was calling her and waved not realising the girl who played Rosie Webster in the soap was behind her. As Vera walked forward with her arms out, focussing on the actress Rosie, our Rosie rushed into the embrace, knocking the unsuspecting actress over.

Security guards came at alarming speed from nowhere and the whole incident was thoroughly embarrassing—well for Rosie anyway, it was hilarious for the rest of the ladies. To be fair, Vera was great once she was untangled from Rosie and Marie explained she had special needs and didn't get out much. The actress signed Rosie's entrance brochure and spoke clearly and slowly to her for a while about nothing much while Rosie was too embarrassed to say anything. That hardly compared to seeing a ghost and finding a murdered person. No comparison really.

Rosie made tea for everyone and brought it through to the main library where Marie and Steph were checking books (sitting in front of a section of books and 'checking' they were in the right order). She put the drinks on the stool they used to get to the highest books.

"Here we go my lovelies, a nice hot cuppa to start the morning after the night before; well day before really I suppose. I don't know about you two but I had a crazy night's sleep, I kept waking up and thinking someone was in the room. I'd jump up and turn the light on but of course there was no one there. Then I'd fall asleep and dream about being trapped behind the library! I hardly slept a wink and I'm thoroughly knackered today".

The other two nodded, Steph said "I dreamt I was stuck in a coffin with a dead body and couldn't get out. The body was top and tail with me and it had hold of my ankle; when I woke up I had somehow got one of my legs caught in Nigel's pyjama bottom's and he was trying to get me out.

Apparently I had already kicked him in the face once which was why he was holding a pillow in front of his face when I woke up. Very surreal." She looked thoughtful and a little puzzled.

Marie patiently waited for the appropriate pause after Steph's story before she started hers. "How bizarre; we all had bad dreams then. I dreamt I was underneath the library with loads of rotting corpses all around me and I could see Ashlea at the top of a hole with a ladder chatting to a young policeman. I kept calling out to her to drop the ladder down to me but she couldn't hear me, I could just see her chatting and laughing with the policeman. Horrible, I was glad when the alarm went off" Rosie nodded slowly looking thoughtful. "Well to be fair, apart from the rotting corpses, yours is the most realistic, Ash does go deaf to anything you say when handsome young policemen talk to her." They all laughed and it soothed the atmosphere which had become a little tense while they were sharing their dreams.

They checked the books in silence for a few minutes, the only sound in the library was when one of them took a book out and slid it back in its rightful place. Rosie spoke first "I suppose after what we went through yesterday it would have been more unusual not to have a bad dream. I mean, it doesn't mean anything, just that we had a memorable experience and our brains were reacting to it. Actually I might have a look in that book of dreams in my break, see what it says."

Marie looked curiously at Rosie who was looking absorbed in her thoughts about her dream's meaning. "I don't know about a book of dreams Rosie, I can't imagine you will find any reference to seeing a ghost and finding a body to liken it to.

However, I might check out that non fiction book about seeing ghosts to see if it has anything in it which could help us communicate with Barry and find out what or who killed him" Marie jumped up to go book hunting.

Steph and Rosie looked alarmed "No" Steph gasped "don't mess with the supernatural Marie, we could end up haunted or with a poltergeist or any number of things could go wrong. No absolutely not, we should leave it to the proper authorities" she emphatically shook her head at the same time.

"Got it!" shouted Marie from between the stacks, brandishing a book called 'Communication with the grave' she looked triumphant. "What? Sorry what did you say?" she said looking at Steph. "I said absolutely no . . . . Oh never mind, bring that book over here and lets have a look."

Marie brought the book to where they were sitting and they moved the mugs so they could open the book where they could all see it. They turned the pages gingerly till they reached the list of contents, Marie traced the headings down with her pointy perfectly polished nail. "The Burning Question', 'An Unanswered Question', 'Who Killed You?' oh that's perfect! Quick, its page seventy three."

Steph carefully turned the pages, a habit borne of many years loving books and libraries—but a bit irritating if you are in a hurry. Marie grabbed a chunk of pages and got to seventy three in a second "Here we go" she said triumphantly, ignoring Steph's obvious irritation.

"Oh, looks like you have to use an Ouija board. Mmm don't really fancy that, Merch will kill me if I accidentally raise a demon who then follows me home and trashes the house. Mind you, it also says if you have already contacted the spirit, you could use the same place to try again. It's got a load of crap in there about burning different herbs and incense and such and chanting the person's name. We could give that a go, we could use Rosie's incense sticks at lunch time and see if we can conjure up Barry again" Marie looked around at the others hopefully.

Rosie looked decidedly uncomfortable "Actually I was saving those incense sticks, and I'm not sure we should be messing about in the occult anyway—especially at work." She frowned at Marie who was obviously disappointed. "Rosie! What the hell were you saving the sticks for?? What special occasion calls for jasmine scented incense sticks? You are just being a scaredy cat again. We'll do it in our lunch break so we won't be wasting anyone's work time, the library will be shut and no harm will come of it. Oh come on Rosie; let's just give it a go?" Marie wheedled, but Rosie was not going to be swayed by Marie again. "I'm not scared; I am simply trying to be sensible. Yesterday we saw Barry's ghost, I just don't think I am ready to unleash any more undead spirits into the library. I have to face the fact that ghosts exist, I don't have to try and attract their attention to me. I was quite happy having no knowledge whatsoever of the 'other world' and I can quite quickly slip back into that blissful ignorance thank you very much!" This was unusually emphatic and forceful for Rosie. Steph and Marie looked at her; she was quite flushed and obviously upset, Marie immediately felt guilty. "OK, ok, don't get your knickers in a twist, it was just a thought. Maybe you're right; we can leave it to the police."

She put her arm round Rosie "Come on hun, lets get the books ready for family reading group" and she led Rosie off towards the children's section to find some books on the history of Birmingham.

Steph picked up the mugs and the book Marie had left on the stool; she carried them all out to the kitchen and dropped the mugs in the bowl. She was just about to walk back in to the library, ready to open up when she looked at the book in her hand.

She had to admit to being intrigued by the whole, communicate with ghost's thing.

Not that she would do anything on her own, but the following Wednesday Steph knew she and Marie were in on their own for the day. She popped the book in her locker and decided to bring it out casually when they were settling down to their morning cuppa the subsequent Wednesday.

As it happened, Steph forgot all about the book in her locker and the library ladies carried on about their normal business for the next two weeks.

They didn't forget what had happened, and spoke about it regularly, especially as the borrowers flooded in to try and find out what had happened. The library ladies enjoyed a level of celebrity they had never experienced before. It lasted for a week or so and then it quietened down and the whole thing seemed like a very distant memory.

There was no news about the body or the murder and even the people coming into the library had stopped asking if they knew anything.

The whole thing was a bit of an anti climax and the ladies were sitting in the closed library on Thursday morning when Ashlea came dashing in. They all looked up, not too concerned by Ashlea's showy entrance; she always tended to arrive everywhere that way.

She had read somewhere that people who made dramatic entrances and first impressions were more likely to be successful, so she did it all the time, just in case the one time when she needed it, she forgot. "They're scaling down the investigation!" She announced evidently scandalised.

The ladies looked perturbed for a second or two, not really knowing what she was referring to. "I went out with PC Davies last night—the bloke that took my number on the day we found the body. He said they think Barry might have been killed by the fall over the fence. He said Barry died from a fractured skull and they think he might have been climbing over the fence to get into the big house at the back of the library and break in. They think he may have been a burglar!"

Steph was visibly distressed. "How can they think that? Barry was really quiet and nice; he wouldn't break into someone's house. He spent forty minutes with Mrs Bellard trying to find a book on goldfish depression—there is no way he is a criminal. Was a criminal, I mean."

"How do they explain that he had no tools for housebreaking?" Wendy queried sensibly.

Ashlea shrugged "It seems to me they haven't spent enough time trying to work this one out at all. James said they never truly thought it was murder, so have actually spent two weeks working out how he could have been killed without anyone else being involved. Problem is no one knows Barry or anything about him, so even though he hasn't got a record or anything, this is easier to put in the report."

Wendy looked very disapprovingly at that comment. "Ashlea, the police wouldn't just make something like this up, they must have investigated very thoroughly and come to this conclusion. Perhaps Sergeant Roberts will pop in later and clear it up for us. Your young PC probably doesn't have access to confidential information that Daniel will have." Ashlea looked untroubled by Wendy's gentle reprimand "He's not my PC, and I couldn't go out with him again anyway. He chewed his food so noisily I kept having to ask him to repeat what he was saying and as soon as he did I had to wipe bits of his food off my dress! Definitely no second date!"

Marie shook her head and curled her lip in disgust. "They cannot believe that Barry was a criminal. He was so quiet, just him and his guinea pig, staying in all the time except when he was at work. What would he want more money for? He didn't even have a car, just a push bike. He used it to get to the shops and the local working mans club on a Sunday afternoon! What sort of burglar would he be? He didn't go out at night at all; his eyesight was really bad and he wasn't comfortable out once the light had gone and only on very special occasions would he go out in the evening and then only if he called a taxi!" Marie noticed that everyone was staring at her and realised what she had done.

Steph raised her eyebrows and asked what everyone was thinking "How the hell do you know all that?" Marie blushed and looked a bit self-conscious "Oh. I couldn't just sit back and do nothing. You and Rosie said I couldn't try and contact Barry again so I had to do something. I looked him up on the computer to see what address he had on his library card and went over there on my day off last week. Merch was playing snooker and I had an hour free, so I thought I would just go and have a look. He lived in a downstairs flat in Northfield and I looked through the windows; nothing to see really, loads of books and an empty animal cage. I went round the back and I could see into the kitchen; typical mans kitchen, microwave, fridge, toaster—all very neat. I couldn't see into the bedroom because the curtains were closed, but I can tell you this was not a man living off ill gotten gains, he looks like he lived within his means to me."

Ashlea scowled at her mom "How do you know all the other stuff about him if you only peeped in the windows? The police didn't seem to know all that stuff you said." Marie tried to look innocent and didn't really pull it off. "Well, I was just coming from round the back of the garden when his next door neighbour, Mildred, came out to see what I was up to. Once I had calmed her down and assured her I wasn't a very bad cat burglar bungling about in the daylight making a lot of noise she was very friendly. I told her I used to work with Barry and once I had assured her I was nothing to do with the police, she invited me in for coffee and spilled everything she knew about Barry."

Marie seemed quite pleased to share this coveted information with the others.

"Apparently she had a very bad experience with the police when her Jack Russell bit a traffic policeman when he tried to stop her mounting the pavement on her moped a couple of summer's ago. She had only just passed her test and got the brakes mixed up with the accelerator and rather than crash into an ice cream man, she turned towards the grass embankment at the side of the road, not noticing the traffic policeman walking away with his ice cream and almost crashed into him.

The problem was that Tinkerbell, the dog, was in a basket on the handlebars and as the policeman reached over to steady the bike, she bit him. Tinkerbell that is, not Mildred. She got a bit carried away arguing with the policeman and according to her, there was an extreme miscarriage of justice. She ended up doing community service and fighting not to have her Tinkerbell put down. In the end she promised to keep her in a muzzle, paid a fine and did her time, sort of. So anyway, she wouldn't speak to the police at all. To be honest, she was a little bit obsessive about the whole police thing I was glad to get out of her flat."

Ashlea spoke first, clearly furious "You silly mare! What if she had been the murderer?? You went there without telling any of us? To investigate a bloody murder! What is wrong with you? You're lucky to be alive, don't ever do anything so stupid again. For Gods sake this is real life mom, anything could have happened. And you should have told the police as soon as you found out all those things; how can they do a proper investigation when dotty old birds like Mildred keep important information from them to get revenge for upsetting her bloody dog?"

She was very red by now and no one was going to interrupt her. Of course they all agreed that she was right, which was also a good reason to keep quiet.

Ashlea and Marie were well known for their near perfect mother daughter / best friends relationship and fiery, honest speaking red hot temper's, so the others stayed quiet.

"Well we can all be analytical and cautious with the benefit of hindsight cant we? I thought I was just going to have a quick look at his home, I didn't know I would bump into his neighbour and she would be all giving all telling did I? I just couldn't pass up an opportunity to get clues like that could I? On reflection perhaps I should have told one of you, but I didn't want to worry anyone." she looked innocent again, but in reality although she hadn't fully thought out possible consequences, she had not told anyone because she wanted to go on her own.

It seemed a bit daft now, but she wanted to come back with essential clues to share with the group and spark everyone's interest again. She imagined herself a young Miss Marple crossed with Shelock Holmes solving the mystery all by herself. By the faces of those around her, they were not satisfied with her answer. Wendy carefully phrased her sentence "Marie, whilst we all love your innovative way of solving problems within the library and indeed your creative ways outside of the library. This is not an occasion where you can solve the problem by yourself and come swaggering back into the library to impress us all. Under no circumstances must you do anything to do with this case alone again or I will have no other option than to tell Merch". That left Marie feeling well and truly told off. She had the grace to blush. "Sorry, you are all absolutely right and my bad, I wont do anything else on my own again.

I promise. But you have to admit, we now have information that means the police are definitely wrong to assume Barry got himself over that fence with the intention of breaking into the big house. He is an innocent victim and no one is going to do anything about it unless it's us." She looked pleadingly at the others. "Ash, when you say scaling the investigation down, did PC whatsit say what that meant—how many people involved now?"

Ashlea looked thoughtful "Well, he just said scaling it down. But earlier he had said there were only two people working on it in the first place once the forensic evidence came back. They said the trolley coin was probably just thrown over the fence and is nothing to do with the body and they didn't find any evidence of anyone else. Well except of mom, and apparently they had ruled her out as a suspect on day one."

Strangely Marie felt a twinge of disappointment that they would rule her out so quickly but said "There you are then, there is a maximum of one person still on the investigation and no one expects to find anything. We know that the trolley coin was his because it was in his hand; we can't just let his murder go un-investigated.

We have to do something because no one else is." She looked resolutely at the others.

The ladies were quiet, none of them had much of an appetite for getting involved in investigating in the murder business, but they had to admit the injustice of an innocent victim and a dastardly murderer going free jarred with their consciences. Rosie spoke first "Marie's right, we can't just let Barry's murder go unpunished. Not only that but poor Barry's reputation is being tarnished by the police saying he died as he was about to commit a crime. I couldn't sleep knowing I've done nothing".

Steph nodded in agreement "I hate to say it out loud, but I agree with both of you. We have to at least try and find out what happened." Wendy and Matilda looked at each other as if silently making a pact and nodded.

Matilda looked excited "Oh I feel like I'm in a Famous Five book out to have a jolly adventure. We will need flasks and sandwiches!" she raised her voice and put a pretend posh accent on whilst pointing to the sky. Ashlea held her hand up "Hold on, you don't know what you're doing yet. If we are seriously going to try and investigate this crime, we have to do it properly. We need to sit down and try to piece together the information we have, like they do in Crimewatch. We need a big whiteboard or flip chart and start mapping out what information and clues we have."

The others looked impressed and Marie glowed with pride. Steph went into the office to get the office chair and Wendy followed her to collect the flip chart. Rosie sorted out different coloured markers and Matilda put the kettle on and opened a packet of custard creams. Within a few minutes they were sitting in front of the flip chart and Ashlea was standing ready to write whatever they came up with on the paper. Rosie had turned the book delivery box upside down, so unusually, everyone had a seat. She dipped her biscuit in her tea after gently tapping it on the table to shake off loose crumbs.

"Well, we should do a spider chart with Barry in the middle and lines leading off to the different elements, like work, home, known associates and so on."

Ashlea dutifully started drawing circles lines and speech bubbles and writing "Right Barry here in the middle. Down here, the trolley coin.

Over here the murder scene and up here his work place. Shall I put Northfield library or West Heath?" she turned to ask her avid audience. "Both" said Wendy and Steph "OK" mused Ashlea drawing another bubble. "What about the neighbour? Was her name Martha?" "Mildred" Marie said muffled by a mouthful of biscuit. "Don't forget the Tinkerbell connection?" said Matilda "She may be linked to this and you should put everything down until you can discount it."

Ashlea looked a bit hesitant "I will write it down, but to be honest the chance of a Jack Russell killing a grown man and throwing him over a six foot fence are slim to say the least. But just in case it is connected, it's there." She wrote it down.

They all sat quietly reading what was written. It wasn't much, just a few words scattered about in circles. It didn't seem so easy now they were actually trying to work out what to do next. For a couple of minutes no one said anything, the only sound was people stirring their tea or tapping their biscuits.

"Look, I know you were worried about the whole communicate with a ghost thing, but I can't see us getting anywhere without a bit more help from Barry. How about we try and get him to come back one more time to give us another clue?" Marie looked imploringly from face to face. "What do you say?" she prompted tentatively sounding desperate now. Still no response from the others, they all sat or stood reflecting on what she had said.

Steph stood up and moved to her locker "Actually, we could have another look at this book and see if there is a nice simple way to call him."

Marie smiled eagerly "You! You kept that book out, no wonder I couldn't find it last week when I came in. How about you Rosie, are you Ok with this?" Marie was acutely aware of how upset Rosie had been last time they discussed this, it had been the reason Marie hadn't tried anything spiritual.

Rosie brushed her hands down her trousers as if she was sweeping something off them, then she stood up and looked as if she had resolved a big problem.

"No, I don't want to do this, but it's not about me, it's about finding out what happened to Barry and if he is the only one that knows, we'll have to give it a try. I'll get those incense sticks". She moved decisively to her locker and fished around for the packet of sticks.

Ashlea, Wendy and Matilda had no idea what they were talking about because they weren't at the library when the original conversation took place. Matilda was used to it, she could rarely keep up with all the conversations and goings on and was about to let it all go on anyway, but Ashlea said "What are you all on about? Communicate with Barry? Isn't Barry dead? I'm confused; you don't all really believe we can talk to his ghost do you?"

Wendy shook her head as if she pitied Ashlea, "Ash you weren't here; none of us believed in ghosts except Matilda. But we all do now, and if he shows up again, you will be a convert too" Ashlea's face said she clearly thought they were all simple and she would never be convinced, but she thought there was no harm in them doing whatever they were going to do with the incense sticks.

"Right, move all the chairs into a circle round the table so we can hold hands and put the incense sticks in the middle." Marie instructed from inside the book waving her free hand randomly around "we need to hold hands and think of Barry, picturing him as clearly as we can. Then we all have to chant his full name. We should really be burning thyme and witch hazel, but those sticks will have to do. If Barry wants us to help us solve this crime I'm sure he'll come, hopefully he is not too far away". They all pulled their various seating arrangements round and joined hands Ashlea and Rosie having to share the table as a seat.

"Should we switch off the lights?" asked Ashlea mysteriously. Matilda smiled and said "Don't be daft Ash, we wont be able to see the ghost if we're sitting in the dark".

They all closed their eyes. Ashlea waited until last in case this was all a piss take and she would end up the laughing stock.

Quietly at first they started chanting 'Barry Thomson, Barry Thomson, Barry Thomson' then instinctively they became a little louder and more insistent 'Barry Thomson, Barry Thomson" after six or seven times they all became quiet but kept hold of each others hands and their eyes remained shut. No one gave a signal to stop but they all just felt it was enough; they all stopped at the same time. Ashlea and Rosie opened their eyes slowly. "What a load of crap. We are the most bonkers bunch of people in Birmingham. Thank

God no one saw us, of course nothing's happened" Ashlea sounded relieved, unhanded her mom and Rosie and wiped her sweaty palms on her jeans.

They all opened their eyes and looked around. Nothing had happened. The rest of the ladies let go of each others hands and Matilda started coughing "If it's not going to bring a ghost, can we put the smelly sticks out; they're stinging my eyes and irritating my chest". Wendy picked the incense sticks up and took them into the kitchen to put them out leaving a trail of jasmine smelling smoke behind her. She called from the kitchen. "These are ruined Rosie, you wont be able to re light them, I've had to put them in the water to stop them smoking." There was no response from Rosie.

In fact there was total silence from the room. When she slowly turned round suspiciously the others were staring at the door to the toilet.

"Oh my God" whispered Ashlea who was as white as a, well a ghost and staring with her mouth gaping open and her eyes like saucers. Wendy knew Barry's ghost was back. She stood still with her back against the sink. She didn't really want to go back into the room, preferring to stay in the kitchen and watch the activities from a safe distance.

Marie spoke first, her voice shaking "The police think you died trying to break into the house behind the library, but we think you were a victim of murder. Who's right Barry?" Nothing happened; Barry's grey figure just floated unmoving in the same spot as he had appeared last time.

Steph whispered to Marie behind her hand; "Perhaps he can't speak. Maybe he might be able to nod or shake his head. Ask him questions that only needs a yes or no answer." Marie nodded slowly "Good idea." She said quietly to Steph, then louder to Barry—the way people speak to someone who speaks another language.

"Barry, were you murdered?" A second or so passed before Barry nodded slightly. A collective intake of breath sucked Wendy back into the room. It was no good, she was missing too much. "Do you know who your murderer was?" Again Barry appeared to think about his response before he nodded. "Ooh who was it Barry" asked Matilda fidgeting with anticipation. No response. "Can you give us a clue Barry, a clue to help us find out who it was and bring them to justice?" Marie asked genuinely. Barry remained motionless for a couple of seconds then floated through the wall.

"Oh great, we're no further forward and he's gone ho." Before Steph could finish her sentence, Barry floated back into the room. They all sat transfixed but nothing else happened. "Was that the clue Barry?" Steph whispered. Barry nodded and floated through the wall again, this time he didn't come back.

Marie stood up on slightly wobbly legs, smoothing her dress and feeling herself in charge of the investigation "Where's he gone then?"

She slowly walked into the hall and was gone for a minute before she came back into the room with the others. She sat back down but looked puzzled, "That wall just goes into the cleaners' cupboard".

Ashlea stood gamely up and wrote 'cleaners cupboard' on the flip chart in red "Well it might be a puzzle, but of all the things on this list at least we know this definitely has something to do with Barry's death." She stood still for a moment, the reality of what had just happened hitting her and causing her to take stock of the situation. She flopped down on the office chair recently vacated by Wendy. "I can't believe I just saw a ghost." She held out her hand "I'm shaking like a leaf, look at me.

How are you all so calm? I feel vomity." Matilda leant over and patted her knee, "Well, it's not so new for us dear, we've already seen Barry. I've seen him four times now, so its almost like seeing one of the regular library users to me, although to be honest, some of our library users are scarier than Barry's ghost and considerably less approachable" Steph spat her tea out as she laughed at Matilda.

Marie went over to Ashlea and gently stroked her hair "Don't worry hun, it will pass, its just shock. Drink your tea and have a custard cream and you'll feel loads better." She turned back to the others whilst still standing protectively beside Ashlea "She's right though, we have to try and find a connection between the cleaner's cupboard and Barry." Rosie nibbled her little finger nail and looked pensive.

"You know, that new cleaner might know something. He comes in to clean before we get here in the morning and he definitely uses the cleaning cupboard. Do any of you know him better than I do? I've only met him once when he had his induction and was introduced to us all; I haven't seen him since and I don't remember much about him"

"His name is Darren and he started here about eight months ago. He came through the agency; I think it's called "Clean Us Up" based in Northfield. He's very good though, the kitchen sink has never been as clean as it is lately; goodness knows how he got all the old stains off. I've met him a couple of times after the initial interview, he's a bit quiet, but very conscientious. I think he cleans at Tesco over the road as well after he's been here in the morning—or maybe he cleans there at night I'm not sure" Steph contributed obligingly.

Marie's eyes opened so wide it looked like they might pop out "Can you hear yourself? He works here AND at Tesco!" The others looked a bit bewildered like they were waiting for a non existent penny to drop. "Honestly, you lot; that's the connection! Tesco trolley coin?? Cleaners cupboard??" Rosie and Ashlea slapped their hands over their mouths at the same time and sucked in a sharp breath.

Steph looked troubled "You think Darren is the connection? You're saying Darren's the murderer?"

Wendy stood up and raised her hands like she was defending herself from attack, "Now don't get carried away, just because Darren works here and at Tesco doesn't mean he's the murderer. That's a mighty jump! He won't have even met Barry.

He's gone before any of us start work; we can't jump to conclusions like that. This is a person's life we're talking about. Those kind of statements start rumours and those kind of rumours can do all sort's of damage, so calm down a bit and take a breath. We have to try and work out what Barry meant; perhaps Darren saw something or perhaps the murder weapon is in the cleaner's cupboard, there could be lots of reasons why Barry went into the cleaner's cupboard."

"Right, fair enough Wend, good call. We don't want to get too carried away.

First things first, someone needs to speak to Darren to find out covertly if he knew Barry or if he knows anything about his murder. How can we do that without raising suspicion? That's especially important if he really has got something to do with this?"

Marie was trying to establish control again, she didn't want everyone to drift off into random discussions or lose focus on what they had to do. Neither did she want them to get so scared or worried about Darren that they decided not to do anything.

"Steph, what time does he come in to clean the library?" she asked. Steph looked up as if to search inside her head. "I think he starts about seven o'clock in the morning and works for about an hour a day, so he should be gone from here by about eight." Steph answered. She looked like she hadn't finished and picked at one of her curls the way she does when she is conflicted or concerned. "Actually, I remember once a few months ago I had to go on a course in town and I had forgotten to take my paperwork home with me the night before. I came here first to pick it up. I got here about half seven. I knew Darren was in the back, I could see the light on and the shutters were half up. I made quite a lot of noise because I didn't want to scare him when I went into the office and as I got half way up the library he came out to see what the noise was. He did look a bit nervous and now I think about it he was a bit short with me, he said 'what are you doing here? You're too early, what time is it?' he was quite a bit snappy. I told him about the course work and the course and he said 'where's your stuff then?' and I said in the office and started walking towards him. He moved backwards towards the staff room and said he was cleaning the sink with chemicals so best if I didn't go in there. I just smiled and said how lovely the sink always looked now and said I would be going once I got my stuff out of the office, I felt a bit like an intruder. He looked relieved and at the time I wondered if he had been asleep and was scared I would see he hadn't done any cleaning because he kind of stood in front of the staff room door. Maybe this is my mind amplifying the incident because he's a suspect, but thinking back he definitely seemed off."

The others now looked intrigued "So now we all agree, he feels like a proper suspect, but how can we get to talk to him? We can't phone him or go to his house. Actually, thinking about it we could do with seeing him here, to be safe. What reason could we have for coming here that early and getting into a conversation with him that seems natural and manages to include a discussion about the body? It would have to be more than one of us too, just in case he has got something to do with it."

Marie waited for someone to come up with something at the same time as turning over ideas in her head. They all sat in silence contemplating the possibilities and desperately trying to think of a solution.

Just then there was a loud bang on the side door which alarmed them all. "Oh my goodness" Wendy exclaimed jumping up at the same time as pointing to the clock "It's five past one and we haven't opened up.

The borrowers are knocking on the door. We've got too carried away with this now and forgotten our actual jobs!

Right, forget this lot for now and Rosie, you go and unlock the door while I get the cash from the office."

Everyone jumped into action and charged into the library to their respective posts and started greeting the grumpy borrowers who had been standing outside for ten minutes. "You lot been asleep? I've been outside since five to one and its bloody freezing. My bladder can't cope with that kind of delay" berated a disgruntled looking old man. "So sorry Mr Bingham, we were intent on a very important task in the office and the clock had stopped" said Steph with her fingers crossed behind her back to cover for the lie "perhaps you would like to use the staff toilet on this occasion to save any embarrassment". She offered.

"No thank you, I'm very fussy about where I wee. I'm only here because I left my false teeth in the World War one section on Tuesday. You bloody close all day Wednesday and now you can't be bothered to open on time today. Not that you lot care, but I haven't been able to eat anything solid for two days!" Marie pulled a face of a person feeling unjustly told off. "Mr Bingham, why did you take your teeth out in the library in the first place?" she enquired politely. "Because they're too big and they keep falling out! I put them on the shelf in the place I took the book out so I didn't lose them, but then when I borrowed the last book I forgot to get the teeth back" he snapped and stomped off into the non fiction section. Marie snort-laughed and tried to hide behind the paperbacks and Ashlea giggled "I'm off now then. It's been an incredible morning, but I don't want to spend any more of my day off here. I'm going shopping to Redditch and I'll pick Dan up from work on the way back. I'm going to an 80's fancy dress tomorrow night for Nade at works birthday, so I'll get into my outfit for your opinion. I'll pop in here just before you close to see if we can come up with a plan to tackle this cleaner. What's his last name? I'll ask Dan if he knows him." "I'll have to check in the office" Steph offered "I think its Mann, but I'm not sure. I can't believe your brother will know him though, I don't think he's from around here even if he lives here now. Worth asking though I suppose, I'll text you his last name if it's not Mann." Marie puckered up for a kiss. "Have a nice time shopping, don't spend too much"

CHAPTER FOUR

The rest of the afternoon passed in a comfortable haze of people wandering in and out of the library, chatting and browsing and generally enjoying the freedom of having free books to choose from and friendly people to chat to in a warm place. Family reading group went well, none of the children wet themselves and the parents managed to listen to the children reading without breaking out into a fight with each other or the staff, so generally a successful event. There was a fine line to be trodden at family reading groups with various sensitivities to take account of. Some of the children were better readers than others, some had support from home and some didn't. You couldn't assume anything, the library ladies didn't refer to moms or dads or brothers or sisters, or reading at home just in case the child or parent took offence or burst into tears due to tragedy unknown to the library staff.

By six thirty the library had quietened down enough for the ladies to group together by the counter. They watched for any borrowers that came in, but by and large focussed on eating chocolate mini eggs and trying, unsuccessfully to come up with a way to get into a conversation with the cleaner without seeming too suspicious.

Marie logged onto her work email to catch up on any messages from the other libraries; the screen lit up with a long list of new emails. She read the first couple and frowned. "Has someone sent an email from my account to all the other Birmingham libraries?" she asked, clearly puzzled by what she had read. Matilda put her hand up; obviously pleased with herself "Mee" she sang cheerfully looking very excited.

"Steph asked me to email the other libraries a warning about Mr Lawrence. He is pretty poorly at the moment and he was behaving very strangely when he came in on Monday apparently"

Steph nodded, her mouth full of mini eggs "Mmm, he uses quite a lot of other libraries, he's bi polar and he's got other mental health issues. You can always tell when he's not taking his medication. He was definitely seriously off yesterday; he was shouting at the paperback stand and got quite aggressive when I asked him to stop because it was upsetting the other customers. He has been very bizarre in the past causing some real problems in Northfield and Bartley Green, so I thought I had better warn the other libraries to keep an eye out for him"

Marie looked exasperated "I have thirteen emails from other libraries asking what I meant by 'very erotic behaviour'! Matilda, the sent email says 'look out for this man, he came into West Heath library today and was acting very erotically'. Honestly, didn't you read it before you sent it?" Matilda shook her head inoffensively.

"I spell checked it just like you showed me. It must be broken." She held her hands out as if the whole thing was beyond her control. "Of course it let this word go through Matilda, it is a real word! It will only pick up words that are spelt wrong and aren't proper words. It's going to take me ages to contact all these people and try to explain what you actually meant—and one of them is from the regional manager! Did you have to use my email?" Marie had her head in her hands moaning dejectedly when Ashlea bounced into the library. The door swung open and the ladies all looked up; standing there Ashlea was dressed as a red crayola crayon. No one spoke for a couple of minutes and Ashlea stood waiting to be appreciated.

Wendy spoke first "Wow, you look em well you look ah just like a giant red wax crayon." Ashlea smiled and walked towards the counter, quite slowly as she could only take very small steps "What do you think?" she asked smiling with self satisfaction. Steph frowned "I thought it was an 80's fancy dress party". Ashlea looked immediately deflated "Oh no, didn't they have crayons in the 80's?" Steph snorted and sprayed chewed up bits of mini eggs on the books she was repairing.

"Yes they had crayons; sorry what was I thinking. Its great, really, you look just like a giant red crayon" she was giggling but trying to control it.

Ashlea wriggled herself round to the desk where they were sitting and lifted up a small red shiny heart shaped handbag "Be honest" she said "Does this bag make me look stupid?" The ladies all tried to stifle their laughter, but it was mostly unsuccessful and Marie tried to rescue the situation as well as she could, she put her arm round

Ashlea, carefully missing the large red pointed cap "No Ash, the bag definitely doesn't make you look stupid"

This created another wave of giggles and snorts from the others. Ashlea smiled widely, paying no attention to the giggling snorting spitting ladies. She was used to them making no sense to her and presumed they were just being barmy as usual.

She dipped her hand in the mini eggs "Good. So what's the plan then?" she looked expectantly at the ladies.

"We haven't come up with one yet. It's been busy in here today and family reading group ran over by twenty minutes.

Daniel and Emma's dad forgot to come with them and he was supposed to take Claire home afterwards as well because her mom is at work. We had to entertain them for a bit while Wendy tracked down the phone number for him. Luckily he had his mobile on him while he was at the bingo or they would still be here!" Steph was shaking her head as she explained the incident—she knew about hopeless dads.

"The problem is how can we get to speak to Darren with more than one of us here without it raising any suspicion?" Steph explained unnecessarily. Ashlea looked thoughtful then put one finger in the air demonstrating that she had an idea, "A staff meeting! You should invite him to a staff meeting early one morning." She looked pleased with herself and dug into the mini eggs again. "But we rarely have staff meetings and the cleaner's are never invited. The cleaners aren't usually interested in book and budget stuff." Pointed out Wendy.

"Shame on you Wendy! I think you should actually ask the cleaner before you decide they aren't interested in books and budgets, I'm surprised at you generalising like that!" Chastised Ashlea. "However, for our current situation you could say to him that once a year the cleaner is invited to make them feel like they are part of the team.

We do it where I work for a staff conference once a year, but there's not enough of you for that and it would take too long to organise. What do you think?" Ashlea looked very pleased with herself.

Marie was nodding "Good idea princess. Steph, you can leave him a message so he gets it in the morning and invite him to one—what day should we say? It can't be Saturday because he doesn't work at the weekend."

She scrunched her face up to emphasise how much she was thinking "How about Monday? That gives us the weekend to organise an agenda and make it look like its normal" she looked around for approval from the others. "Ok" agreed Steph decisively "I'll tell him he doesn't have to clean on Monday, but to come in at eight so we can have the meeting before the library opens. Can everyone make it into work for Monday at eight?" Matilda looked a bit distressed. "I don't usually get up till eight; I don't think Gerald will like it if he has to get me here that early, especially as I shouldn't be working at all. You might have to have it without me". Wendy looked concerned for her, "Don't worry Matilda, we'll fill you in when you get here." She smiled encouragingly at her.

Wendy coughed artificially, "I can come in early, but I might have to leave a bit early or have a longer lunch; Mark worries about me working too much, he thinks I should put my feet up more. I'm a martyr to my veins as you know if I spend too long on the go." Marie sighed pointedly obviously unimpressed by Wendy's speech "Don't worry Wend, me Steph and Rosie can close up on Monday, so you can go half an hour early ok? We're not martyrs to any part of our bodies although Rosie is a martyr to port" Rosie giggled and pushed Marie playfully.

"Not a martyr to port at all, port and I are just very close friends. I'm ok though, Mick is on lates on Monday so he can take the kids to school. I wouldn't miss this for the world." Ashlea pulled a face as she realised she would be on the way to work on Monday at eight. "Damn it, I suggested it and I won't be able to be here. You'll have to email me to let me know what happens"

Rosie assured her "I can do that, I'm in the office Monday morning. Did Dan know Darrens name Ash, had he heard of him?" Ashlea looked pensive like she was reluctant to speak (highly unlikely) "Actually he thought he did, but I think he must have the wrong one. The guy he was describing didn't sound like he'd be a very good library cleaner. He said one of the lads in the football team got some designer drugs off a Daz Mann a few months ago in the pub on Kings Norton Green. Apparently they made him really ill and he was in a coma in hospital for a few days. He said that this Daz Mann is about twenty five to twenty seven, black curly hair and skinny, but none of them have seen him since he sold the stuff to Chet".

Steph rubbed her chin with one hand and curled a strand of her hair with the other looking contemplative "Worryingly that does actually sound a bit like our Darren. He is late twenty's, very slim and has short black curly hair. I just can't believe he is a drug dealer; the agency always does a CRB check so he can't have a criminal record and he had really good references. And you have to admit he is a brilliant cleaner, surely if he was dealing drugs he wouldn't need the cash". Wendy stood up brushing down crumbs and bits of chocolate shell off her lap. "Well we should find out one way or the other on Monday, so let's not worry about it now its time to close up."

She started walking round the library to check there was no one hidden in any of the corners or between the book stacks.

They had to be extra vigilant to make sure that they didn't accidentally lock anybody in the library at closing time, ever since the time when the police had called Steph to come and open the library at four o'clock in the morning last summer.

Apparently the ladies had been less than thorough when they did the check round that night and they dashed out turning off all the lights and putting the metal shutter down, not realising old Mr Bellamy was fast asleep on a children's chair in the non fiction section. The alarm wasn't working, as usual, which when you consider Mr Bellamy had a weak heart, for once was probably a good job.

He woke up, panicked thinking he'd gone blind because it was so dark, and then spent almost an hour banging on the walls to try to attract attention outside. Finally he felt his way to the counter, found there was a phone on the desk and phoned 999. All the ladies got into trouble for that and none of them mentioned that their urgent need to get out was because they had an invite to the policeman's ball at TallyHo training centre. None of them complained at having to clear up three puddles of wee either. At least Mr Bellamy was good as new after staying with his daughter in Weston Super Mare for a couple of weeks. Although sadly he had not been back to the library since.

"Right all clear" called Wendy, "Lock it up girlies, time to go home" she almost skipped down the library to get her stuff from the staff room.

She always cheered up at home time, Mark nearly always had a mug of tea and some dinner waiting for her and she only had to mention her aching feet and he whipped the baby oil out for a lovely foot massage. She could feel her arches relaxing just thinking about it.

Matilda called out "Night ladies, I'm off now, Gerald is outside and I forgot I was supposed to go out at six thirty so he could be back for some politics programme, so he'll be grumpy." she pulled a face as she buttoned up her bright red duffle coat. "Well, why didn't he just come in and get you hun?" Marie asked good-naturedly trying not to notice how much like Paddington Matilda looked as she put up her hood. "Oh he always picks me up in his slippers, so he won't get out of the car no matter what happens. We were stopped by the police not long ago for driving too slow on the Bristol Road. When the policeman asked him to get out of the car he said no!

At first the officer was really uppity, but once Gerald explained that he had his favourite slippers on and he didn't want to ruin them on the wet pavement, the officer calmed down a bit and put his book and pen away. In fact, he sat in the car with us for a bit. It was a filthy night and he was soaking through. He had some tea out of our flask and a cheese sandwich." She looked wistful and dreamy "He was a lovely young man, David; he'd just had his first baby and said I looked a bit like his Nan, who's dead. She used to live in Bourneville before she died and he said her husband, his granddad, was barmy as well. Said she died on purpose to get away from his flights of fancy; led her a merry dance for years apparently. Mind he was quite firm when he told Gerald he should get up to thirty miles an hour as much as possible on the main roads and suggested he consider wearing shoes or his less favourite slippers in case he had to get out of the car at any point during a journey. Gerald didn't listen to him though—never listens to anybody. Night all." she waved her hand knitted mittens majestically as she disappeared behind the door.

Ashlea shuffled around to Marie to give her a kiss "Right I'm off too, got to meet Daniel outside. He's driving us to see Elliot for a bit cos he's off the beer in the week and I can't really reach all the pedals in this outfit." She waved (from the elbow down) to the others and slipped awkwardly out of the door.

Steph took the cash out to the office to lock away. She punched the code in for the safe and noticed her lovely nails were chipped. She tutted out loud as she shoved the cash bags into the box. She had always had short nails because she nibbled them when she was nervous or concentrating and it had always been a disappointment to her. She loved Marie's nails, always long and perfectly shaped and a rainbow of different colours to match her outfits. So last payday she had decided to have gel nail extensions and she loved them; every time she noticed her own hands ripples of pleasure washed over her and she stopped whatever she was doing to gaze at them transfixed by their loveliness. But they were expensive and now she would have to go and get a repair—bloody safe.

She sat back up on the chair in a huff and noticed her hair in the reflection of the office window. She was strawberry blond and her hair had a natural wave, not always fashionable she knew, but very on trend at the moment. Good job because she couldn't afford nails and hair. She patted it and twisted a curl round her finger and smiled to herself, pleased with her reflection, she was nearly fifty and still pretty and she knew she looked younger than her age—despite having a family intent on sending her into an early grave with worry over one thing or another ten.

She wrote the note to Darren, telling him it was the annual all staff meeting on Monday and he was invited. She wrote that he wouldn't need to clean but needed to come in at eight for the meeting instead. She put in brackets that he would be paid his normal rate so he understood he wouldn't miss out because he wasn't actually cleaning. She folded the note neatly and popped it in an envelope, wrote his name on the front in capital letters and propped it up against the phone on top of the desk in plain sight. She took a deep breath and stood up, flicking the light off in the office. The dark immediately shrouded her and it felt odd, kind of weighty. She looked back into the room, almost expecting to see something there but the office was empty.

She shivered, feeling spooked and quickly headed for the warmth and light of the staff room. She shut the door firmly behind her.

Rosie was already putting her coat on in the staff room quietly humming an unidentifiable tune. She looked up when Steph came in "I cant hang about today either hun, Mick's got the kids but he's got quiz night at the Stone and he's got to be there by half seven. He is their specialist subject person so he can't be late" Steph looked up from buttoning her coat, interested. "What's his specialist subject then? Medical terminology? How to drive an ambulance really quick without crashing? Medicines of the twenty first century? Do tell".

Rosie smiled cheekily at Steph as she pulled her hat on. "Christ knows—I'm sure he told me but for the life of me I can't remember, might have been music, but to be honest I had already drunk three glasses of port by the time he came home, so I just smiled and nodded at everything he said. Anything for a quiet life. If he hadn't text to remind me I would have forgotten all about it."

Steph frowned with her concerned mom face on, "You should be careful with your drinking sweetie, three glasses is a lot in one night." Rosie looked a bit wistful "I know and I don't do it often, but it was our wedding anniversary and just because Mick was at work didn't mean I couldn't celebrate on my own. Mind then just as I was getting maudlin, he turned up with an anniversary present, a lovely sexy nightie. Problem was he bought it in a size ten and I've been a size fourteen for about three years so I ended up crying and having another glass and still no dinner which meant I finished up being sick in the back garden. A miserable night really, but he has promised to make it up to me at the weekend, so fingers crossed" she crossed her fingers in the air to demonstrate how crossed fingers looked.

Steph looked doubtful, "Don't build your hopes up though Rosie, his record for romantic breaks is not exactly Romeo and Juliet worthy is it? I mean his hearts in the right place but that last time in Oxford was really dangerous." Rosie's eyebrows lifted in surprise, "Oh Steph that wasn't his fault. How could he have known the bank would be held up while we were getting our cash out? Even I didn't blame him for that and the police report said he was very brave for trying to trip the robber up on his way past." Steph wasn't impressed and tied her coat belt a bit too tightly to show it. "Fair enough Rosie, but he could have guessed that if he tripped the robber up he would fall directly onto you, and he had a gun! Vigilantism has its place, but that was a bit reckless" Steph took on a lecturing tone and Rosie butted in waving her hand to make Steph stop talking. "Look, that's easy to say, but when you're in those situations you don't think, you just act. He is trained to respond in challenging situations as a paramedic, so he reacted spontaneously and anyway I thought he was really brave. My bruises didn't last long anyway and gave us a great talking point at the readers club; it provoked some lively discussions, so no real harm done. I don't mind what we do anyway, an hour in a café away from the kids would be enough to make my weekend special" she said wryly grinning self depreciatingly. Steph laughed "Swap you mine for yours". "No way" Rosie shook her head adamantly "At least I can send mine to their room when they drive me mad cause they're still small. I couldn't control yours" She waved airily as she went out the door.

"I can't bloody control them either" Steph mumbled to herself as she picked up her hat and gloves and followed her through the door.

Marie was walking down the dark library towards the staff room as the others were walking towards the exit. "Come on you" urged Steph "Wendy; you and Rosie can carry on, I'll wait for Marie and we'll lock up". "Cheers girls" called Rosie "Thanks. Night night" from Wendy who never needed to be told twice when home time was concerned.

Marie was whining as she walked "I had to respond to all those bloody emails. Fancy letting Matilda use my account. What were you thinking Steph?" Steph beamed and didn't look at all sympathetic. "I was logging the new books and everyone else was busy, what can I say? You shouldn't leave your email up; I keep telling you its dodgy not to log out when you're using a shared computer. Besides I dictated to Matilda what to put in the email, how could I know she could still manage to get it wrong" Steph was now talking to the closed staff room door. She shrugged and sat down to wait for Marie.

Marie was bending over getting her handbag out of her locker still mumbling to herself about incompetent people, when she felt a shiver go down her back from her neck. Suddenly all email thoughts were wiped from her mind. She was frightened to move, she could sense something or someone was behind her. She slowly closed her locker and straightened to lean forward to unhook her coat from its peg in slow motion, almost waiting for someone to touch her or speak. Taking a deep breath and holding it she clutched her things close to her chest and very slowly turned round. There was nothing there, she looked around to make sure then she let her breath out and smiled to herself; it was just the empty dark corridor to the cleaner's cupboard and toilet.

Funny though, she thought, it had really felt like she knew something or somebody was watching her. She genuinely thought she would see Barry when she turned round—well she hoped it would be Barry, the last thing they needed now was another ghost.

She smiled at the ridiculousness of her own thinking—another ghost indeed. A slight breeze blew her fringe and made her jump; she glanced cautiously around the room; there was nowhere for air to get in. She quickly grabbed the door handle and hurried down the library to where Steph was waiting to lock up and put the shutter down.

Marie burst through the door into the library and startled Steph. "Blimey Marie you nearly gave me a heart attack! Slow down pet you'll bump into something in the dark and do yourself an injury." Steph cautioned shooting up out of her chair hands in the air. Then she noticed Marie's face, "What's the matter? You look terrified." Marie stopped rushing and took a couple of breaths while slowly shaking her head. "Probably nothing" she gasped. "Just got nervy in the staffroom. I was getting my bag out of the locker when I was sure someone or something was behind me, but when I turned round; nothing. Then there was, like a puff of air that blew my fringe across my face, but there's no window open in there, nowhere for wind to come in." She leaned forward to catch her breath, she hadn't taken a proper lungful of air since she dashed down the library and her lack of fitness meant she was panting heavily. "Sit down a minute and catch your breath before you have a coronary!" Steph manhandled Marie into a chair. "We have had a few very spooky weeks; it's understandable that you are feeling a bit susceptible to these kinds of 'experiences'"

Marie rolled her eyes at Steph "What do you mean 'experiences'? I'm hardly a medium am I? With the Barry thing we were just in the right place at the right time- or wrong time depending on how you look at it. I couldn't face the thought that the staff room has become some sort of short cut to the other side! No, I'm sure it was just me being over sensitive, let's get out of here and get home for some normality." She stood up and wrestled herself into her coat wanting to put as much distance between her and the staffroom as possible.

Normality wasn't really on the menu for any of the ladies that night. Whether it was because they were subconsciously thinking about the murder or the cleaner or whether it was just Thursday night madness, it was a night they would all bemoan when they talked about it afterwards.

Steph got home to find the front door had a broken pane of glass in it and two very loud angry daughters were being dragged into the house by an even angrier dad.

The next fifteen minutes was a solid wall of noise and she didn't even try to work out what had happened. She went into the kitchen, quietly closed the door, made herself a cup of tea and phoned the local Chinese to deliver food. No one noticed she had come home despite her walking past them all, which on one hand was a little demoralising but on the other hand meant that no one expected her to join in with the war that was raging in the living room. So she stayed where she was, sipping her tea and flicking through the free newspaper, not hiding as such, but quietly waiting for the Chinese food to arrive before announcing her presence to her noisy angry family.

Wendy got home to find Mark fast asleep in the chair. No cup of tea and no dinner on. Apparently he had cleaned out the loft, exhausted himself and had been asleep since he dropped their grandson home. Very disappointed Wendy tried not to moan too much. She was not used to having to cook when she came home from work—so it was toast and beans and very stilted conversation. Her tired arches stayed firmly in her slippers.

Matilda was fed up by the time they got home. Gerald had complained for the whole journey about missing his politics programme and when Matilda had tentatively pointed out that if he would speed the car up a bit, they might still make it, he spent ten minutes lecturing her on the danger of speeding traffic and quoting loads of unsubstantiated statistics at her. Her evening was only rescued because Gerald had remembered to switch the slow cooker on and she smelt the lamb stew as soon as she walked in the warm house.

Rosie got home just in time to pass Mick over the door threshold. He handed her a carrier bag and kissed her cheek. "Sorry to dash love, but the quiz captain has already phoned me once, I'm late. Billie's been sick—it's in this bag and Lucy's got nail varnish in her hair and on her school uniform. Back by eleven, see ya" He waved to a stunned Rosie standing on the doorstep with a bag of sick in her hand as Billie walked out stark naked.

"Mom, I've been sick. Oh oh there it is" he pointed at the bag in his moms hand triumphantly; Rosie looked down at him, bewildered "Why is it in a bag Billie?" Billie thought for a minute "I told Lucy I was going to be sick and she got it for me. I was watching Peppa Pig so I couldn't get up" he smiled his most dazzling smile and walked back inside. Rosie followed, bemused but resigned.

Marie felt unsettled all the way home; she was even reluctant to look in the rear view mirror just in case she saw something or someone in her back seat. She pulled onto the drive and the house was in darkness, Merch was obviously out or asleep. She let herself in and turned on all the lights she passed. She checked the lounge but Merch wasn't there. She couldn't kick the feeling of being off kilter somehow. The house seemed so quiet. She walked into the tidy kitchen putting the light on as she went. There was a note on the table from Merch; 'Playing snooker with your dad. See you later xx'. Great, that meant the whole night to herself. Normally that would be a good thing, she would watch something on catch up TV or something she had recorded, paint her nails, have a long soak in the bath. But tonight, she needed company. Tonight she couldn't face being in the creaky empty house all alone.

She fished out her mobile and phoned Ashlea. "Hi hun, are you back home from Elliot's? You doing anything tonight?" she asked hopefully but trying not to sound desperate.

"Yes we're just back, Dan was only poppin up to borrow his football boots and no to doing anything why?" Ashlea responded.

"Can I come and have a cuppa and a cuddle of Sookie? I'll bring chips" She wheedled. She loved Ashlea's puppy Sookie, no matter what kind of a day you had, Sookie made you feel better with her lolloping about and happy bonkersness. "Of course you can come, but I've made cottage pie, so you can have some of that. I'll get the kettle on, see you in a minute" Ashlea said chirpily and hung up.

Suddenly the contrast between Ashlea's happy voice in her ear and the quiet in the house seemed startling. The silence was deafening so she picked up her bag and keys and walked straight out of the door without switching any lights off. She slammed the door and charged to her car knowing it would look to anyone that she was being chased and feeling a bit daft. Oh well, she would feel better in a couple of hours and she could come home and go to bed as normal.

Chapter Five

Friday was a short staffed day; Marie and Rosie were on their own in the morning with Steph coming in after lunch.

The two ladies opened up, dealt with the two people waiting to come in and bring their books back and sat down with a mug of tea to work out a staff meeting agenda. "It's harder than you think. The problem is it's not really our sort of thing is it? We don't do staff meetings unless it is an official one with the people from central library and that's so rare I can't remember anything they ever discuss." Marie said. "What can we say? We need to think of something that affects everyone. Pity its not wage increase time because that would work."

Rosie screwed her nose up deep in thought, "How about the news about the new library building proposal? That affects everyone and even though the plans and that aren't ready yet, its ok that we know about it first isn't it? For twenty years there have been rumours of a new library and now they are actually going to build one—that's got to be worth an agenda item" she sank back into her chair, cuddling her tea and satisfied with her contribution. "Great, well done Rosie" Marie smiled encouraged and started typing "Item one; New Library Proposal. It's a good start.

How about the budget submissions for new books? I know it hasn't been approved yet, but Darren won't know that and at least it sounds official." Rosie nodded in agreement. "Right, item two: Budget Submissions. How soon can we put something in about Barry do you think?" She looked up at Rosie who was just stamping someone's books "Thank you Mrs Jeepers, bye, take care down those steps; they're still a bit slippy".

She sat back down "Not sure hun. We need more on the agenda. How about something about the dirty fridge? No one ever cleans it out and I'm sick of having to scrape the mould off the door and bleach the shelves because people spill stuff and don't clean it up." Marie looked back at the screen and nodded "Ok, that's a local concern so we can have that. Item three: Fridge Maintenance. Now, we need to make it sound official, no one would have an item on an agenda that was just gossip." She paused for a couple of minutes her brain working overtime trying to make something sound realistic in her head before she said it out loud. Then she raised her eyebrows in a self satisfied gesture "How about putting down that the police have updated us and asked us to discuss the issue of the body with other members of staff to see if they have heard anything that could contribute to the investigation?" Marie asked.

Rosie looked a bit troubled, "But the police have told us they are not investigating it anymore, what if he knows that already? I don't want us to get caught out, just in case." Rosie whispered the last bit, even though the library was empty. "Oh don't be so wet" Marie scorned "He's not going to know that is he? We only know because Ashlca went out with that PC. No I think it's worth the risk, item four: Police Enquiry. There, we can finish it off with item five: Any Other Business.

Great that's finished, I'll print out a few copies and we can all have one each on Monday." She pressed the print button flamboyantly and jumped up to go to the printer to retrieve her copies. She came round the table brandishing her pile of documents. "Looks quite professional if I say so myself, and I doubt Darren will have anything to compare it with anyway." She shuffled the paper's like a pack of cards and put them under the till drawer for safe keeping until Monday. "Now, while it's quiet, how about we get started on the Anti Addiction display for next month?

We've got some bright pink play dough to make the giant tablets and I was going to use the plastic sheets and a knitting needle to make a syringe. I've already started the giant cigarette, what do you want to do?"

Rosie had a think before nodding, "The syringe I think, we had better leave the tablets for Steph. They'll be fairly simple to do and easy to repair if she gets them wrong. You know she likes to have a go, but she's not really creative is she?" Marie nodded concurring with Rosie's assessment. "Good choice" and she headed off to the staff room to collect the odd assortment of scrap and crap that made up their display materials.

The weekend passed quickly for all the ladies and they barely had a chance to think about how they would handle the staff meeting or worry about what might happen.

Steph did think about it once or twice, knowing she would be chairing the meeting. Unfortunately with three teenage girls she loved and wanted to leave in equal measure and a husband she mostly wanted to strangle, she didn't have the luxury of planning what she would say. In fact the only luxury she had all weekend was when she went to Sainsbury's and spent an hour wandering round with a trolley collecting shopping. No pressure, no noise and she even sat and had a cup of coffee in the café all by herself reading the supermarket free magazine—heaven.

Wendy completely forgot about the staff meeting within minutes of reaching home. She spent the weekend helping her daughter Kelly with her children, a task she truly loved.

They went out to the park; watched children's television coloured in pictures and sang nursery rhymes while Kelly decorated the bedroom. Mark floated around in the background, helping mother or daughter when required and keeping out of the way when superfluous; he had this down to a fine art due to years of practice. By the time Wendy landed home on Sunday evening she was feeling serene and satisfied.

She only thought about the staff meeting when she set her alarm, abruptly remembering she would need to go in early, but apart from a brief frown, she was unperturbed by the thought—her weekend had been too perfect for anything to do with work to spoil, so she promptly fell into an untroubled and peaceful sleep.

Matilda had a busy weekend. Gerald had booked for them to try dry slope skiing at the Snow Dome in preparation for their skiing holiday in January. Matilda had been a natural, skiing after the briefest of lessons with a lovely young man named Bill; she was off down the slopes on her own.

Gerald was a different matter. Bill spent the whole day with him and he still hadn't managed to build up enough speed to get down the nursery slope once without falling over due to lack of momentum. He became increasingly grumpy and decided that skiing wasn't really his thing and he would be in charge of taking photographs when the holiday came.

Sunday was spent sorting out one of the spare bedrooms. The task took hours as Matilda was a bit of a hoarder and Gerald was very keen on a quiet life, so left her to it.

One good thing about hoarding though was that they had years of interesting things to look at and ended up hardly throwing anything away. They both fell into bed exhausted at ten o'clock with wonderful memories filling their heads and dreams.

Rosie's weekend was exhausting as always. Between ballet dancing for Lucy and Billie, swimming lessons for Billie (Lucy was a good swimmer anyway and took a dislike to the swimming teacher who she said looked like the BFG) a party on Saturday for Billie and one on Sunday for all of them (Aunty Helen's fortieth) she hardly had a moment to brush her teeth let alone worry about work on Monday. She forgot all about the something special with Mick she was expecting to make up for the rubbish anniversary evening. She was so tired by Sunday evening that she went straight to bed once the children were asleep and was snoring lightly by eight thirty. She dreamt of being at a swimming party with all her relatives and some strange looking giants—probably the result of the twix she ate just before she brought the children up to bed mixed with the random party food she had stuffed steadily throughout the day.

Marie went shopping straight after work on Saturday and had a lovely mooch around the supermarket buying the buy one get one's free's and much too much chocolate and sweets. It's always a bad idea to go shopping when you're hungry, especially when you're oozing out of your size twelve's into size fourteen and your wardrobe was full of size twelve's as your significant other was fond of pointing out.

Saturday night was take away night too so no cooking. She put the shopping away and made tea then got undressed into her lounging about the house pyjamas almost immediately. The evening reached the perfect pitch as she cuddled up to Merch on the settee eating her take away and watching Midsummer Murders.

She woke up early on Sunday and while she relished the first few minutes of wakefulness knowing she hadn't got to get up for anything in particular, she decided she would pop into the Tesco opposite the library on the way to visit Ashlea and Daniel (and Sookie of course). If she happened to get chatting to the girls that worked there and ask about their cleaner, so be it. She hopped into the shower with visions of herself cracking the crime and being hailed a hero by the library staff and local police. She sang loudly and decided she would have a cooked breakfast with Merch before she headed off to her investigating.

CHAPTER SIX

Monday morning dawned grey and misty and a damp chill hung in the air. The snow had completely melted away and the world was looking bleak and dreary. As each of the ladies drifted into wakefulness it didn't take long for the reality of what they were about to try to activate butterflies in their stomachs. None of the ladies heading for work that day ate any breakfast. Matilda of course wasn't going in until late and had forgotten about the meeting with Darren until long after her bacon sandwich and second cup of tea.

Steph arrived at the library first and waited in her car outside the front until Marie turned up five minutes later.

She had been faffing around in her glove compartment as if she was doing something, but really she didn't want to go in alone. The shutter was half way up and she could see a light at the back of the library. As Marie got out of her car to walk to meet Steph, Rosie and Wendy came around the corner; so they waited together for them to park and get out of their cars before they headed to the door. They all said fairly subdued good mornings, but nothing more, for whatever reason none of them could think of anything to say.

Once inside Marie put on a slightly too loud falsely cheerful voice "Ooh how lovely to get inside the nice warm library, it's a really chilly day out there." she rubbed her hands together and beat them on the opposite shoulders as if to warm herself up. Rosie looked at her as if she was a little odd (which she was) and said (loudly) "Yes, it is—pity we had to come out at all on a day like this. Shall we have a cup of tea to start with; warm us up before we get onto the meeting?" "Oh lovely idea" said Steph "I have some biscuits. Let's go into the staff room and sort ourselves out before we start the meeting." Steph had spoken equally brightly and with increased volume as she started walking down the library. She turned round and used her head to indicate to the others that they should come with her.

They all walked a little hesitantly down the library to the staff room and stopped outside the door. They looked at each other and down at the door handle but did nothing. Marie tutted and moved to the front, she grabbed the handle, pushed open the door and breezed into the room, holding the door for the others "Come on you lot, cuppa time. Oh morning hun, you must be Darren" she held out her hand casually for Darren to shake "nice to finally meet you".

Darren was standing in the doorway to the kitchen, looking perfectly at ease, almost as if the others were coming into his home. He stepped forward hesitantly the left half of his face covered by a long lank fringe, he took Marie's hand weakly and mumbled "Morning" then stepped back again. Steph smiled at Darren and said "Thank you for coming this morning Darren, this is Rosie" she waved at Rosie "this is Wendy" she waved at Wendy "Finally Marie—just in case you don't remember everyone you have met and I am obviously Steph. We're just going to make a cup of tea to have at the meeting, would you like one?"

Darren looked cautious, he had nodded at each of the woman as they were introduced, but made no move to unblock the kitchen doorway. Steph started moving towards him as if she assumed he would move out of her way.

When he didn't she raised her eyebrows and said "Excuse me, I need to get into the kitchen—and would you like one?" He moved so that Steph could just get past and shook his head. For a minute they all stood in awkward silence listening to tea making noises in the kitchen.

The library was still cold because no heating was used on a Sunday and it took a bit of time for the rubbish central heating to warm the flimsy building up on a Monday morning. This meant no one wanted to take their coats off so there didn't seem to be any reason to move.

Finally Wendy sighed and said "Right, well, shall we go and sort out the seating and give out the agendas?" Rosie and Marie nodded and Rosie appeared to come round from a trance and cheerily she said "Good idea Wendy, I'll bring the biscuits and a note pad, to take notes". They all started walking through the door into the library, Marie going last, she held the door for Darren "Coming?" she asked. He looked like he might not, but then after a long pause and a backwards glance into the kitchen, he started moving towards the door. He followed Marie down to the front of the library where Rosie and Wendy had started setting out some chairs round the table in the children's area and placing an agenda in front of each place on the table.

Without speaking they all sat down just as they heard Steph coming through the library from the staffroom with the tea mugs clinking on a tray. "Here we go; we should always start the day with a lovely cuppa." She arrived with a flourish and started dishing out mugs. She smiled in an over friendly way at Darren, but he didn't smile back.

Steph picked up the agenda from in front of her and cleared her throat. "Thank you all for coming to the meeting so early, and thank you Darren for coming later so that you could attend" she smiled at him again, waiting for him to respond, but he didn't. Her smile faltered but she carried gamely on. "Item one; New Library proposal. Wendy, can you update us from the meeting you went to last week please?" Wendy straightened herself up and blushed as everyone looked her way. "Well, they said the money for the new building for the library up by the community centre has been approved.

The plans have been drawn up so it's a definite proposal now, for the first time in twenty years! They have to do some consultation with local people, but all being well we will have the new library built within about twelve months." Wendy visibly relaxed once she finished speaking. She wasn't fond of public speaking at the best of times and although this was only the ladies and Darren, because it was a proper meeting it felt different, more pressurised than normal and she didn't like it.

Steph smiled encouragingly at Wendy "Well that's really good news isn't it? A new library at last and on a different site so we won't have to close this one until the new one is built, fab. Anyone want to say anything else about that?" She looked around the staff with eyebrows unnaturally high. "No? Right then on to item two; Budget Submissions. I can do this one, although as usual I don't have much to update you with. We put in a budget request for books at five percent higher than last year to allow for publishers price increases, but we haven't heard if we have been successful yet. There have been rumours of cuts to book budgets in the Northfield constituency which could affect us, but I don't think we should worry about it until we hear officially. Our budget submission is always smaller than the other libraries so we might get all of ours. As Wendy said the capital budget to build a new library has been approved, which is the most important thing, but that's it so far. On to item three; Fridge Maintenance? Who added this item to the agenda?" Steph looked enquiringly around at the others.

Rosie nearly fell off her chair as Marie nudged her a bit hard, she had obviously been daydreaming. "Oh right" she said glaring at Marie "That was me.

The fridge is not being looked after properly. Every time I go into it, there is something spilled and not cleaned up. I'm tired of always being the one to clean it up so I think we need a rota." She pulled out an A4 sheet of paper with writing on it from under her agenda. "I prepared this to ensure that everyone cleans the fridge in rotation and I have bought some anti septic wipes to use so it's not too onerous a task."

Marie had her lip curled like Elvis "Really, you feel a rota is absolutely necessary Rosie? You don't think your obsessive need for cleanliness is getting a little out of hand?" Rosie opened her mouth to answer but Steph jumped in spotting potential for friction. "No Marie, I agree with Rosie. We have left it up to individuals to keep the fridge clean and that hasn't worked, so we'll try Rosie's rota" she took the sheet of paper off Rosie, "You can claim back the cost of the wipes from petty cash." Rosie gave Marie a 'I won you lost smirk' and Marie rolled her eyes and shrugged.

"Item four. humph, er the Police Enquiry, who wants to speak to this item?" she looked at the others optimistically. "I will" piped up Marie "This is obviously about the body which was discovered behind the library." She looked directly at Darren who was picking the skin on his fingers and hadn't lifted his head up at any time during the meeting. "Darren, are you aware of the police investigation?" she enquired innocently Darren looked up startled by the sound of his name and flicked his limp fringe up. "What?" he said; Marie smiled indulgently at him. "I said are you aware of the police investigation into the dead body of Barry Thomson which was found behind the library?" He was quiet for a few seconds just sitting with a frozen expression which said nothing about what he was thinking.

Marie was beginning to think he was a bit slow or perhaps hard of hearing. At last he said quietly "Why would I know anything? I didn't know him, I never met him, and the police don't think its anything to do with me" The ladies all looked at him expectantly.

Marie spoke "I didn't say anyone thought it was anything to do with you Darren, I just asked if you were aware of the investigation. Had you noticed anything strange on the mornings when you got here in the week or two before the body was discovered?"

He squirmed in his seat looking down at the floor and picked the skin on his fingers again clearly agitated. "No. I didn't see anything, now I've got to go. I've got another job to go to." he got up and walked determinedly down to the computer area where he had left his outer clothing. He picked up his coat and half put it on then stopped and stood still for a few seconds. He turned fully around frowning to stare pointedly at the group, looking at each of them in turn. "You should leave the murder enquiry alone, the police are paid to do all that investigating stuff. You're paid to do book stuff." His face relaxed; then he walked out of the library pulling his coat on as he went.

Everyone sat staring at the space he had vacated without saying anything for a few seconds. Rosie abruptly leapt up to go and lock the door behind him. The library didn't open for another half an hour but if the door was open it was guaranteed a borrower would walk in no matter what time it was or how dark.

As she came back in her face comic admonished she said "Well, that wasn't altogether successful was it?" Marie put up her hand and raised her eyebrows "Actually I think it was; come on, it's obvious it was him—he was suspicious from the start, furtive behaviour, non communication and then his comment at the end, definitely guilty!" She said this forcefully shaking her head.

"Hang on, he's a teenager—my girls act like that all the bloody time, doesn't mean they're guilty of murder." Steph said passionately.

Then she looked as if she was thinking about her own comment. "Well not actual murder anyway. He could just be shy or a bit simple."

Marie made a noise like a frustrated teenager. "Firstly he's not a teenager, he's in his twenty's and I can't think he's shy or simple; he was warning us off before he left! No I'm certain it was him, we just have to find out why and how. Did I mention that he had been sacked from Tesco's?" The others looked suitably taken aback "No, but how do you know?" asked Rosie. "Well I popped in to do a bit of shopping yesterday on the way to see Daniel and Ashlea and got chatting to the lady on the deli counter. Apparently they caught him on cctv walking out with a big bag of Tesco's own washing powder without paying for it, after work when the shop was shut. They confronted him, and he said he was going to pay, but had forgotten. Unfortunately for him they had him on camera doing it twice two days apart so they felt he had plenty of time to offer to pay. What a daft thing to get sacked for though? Not fags or booze, bloody washing powder and two big bags at that! He must have an awful lot of dirty washing—odd or what? So anyway, he hasn't worked there for just over a week" Marie leant back on her chair, satisfied that she had imparted interesting and vital information to the rest of the team.

Steph looked puzzled "That is odd; why would he steal two bags of washing powder—cheap own brand stuff too. Doesn't make sense, I mean those are definitely the biggest bags of washing powder they sell, but not the most expensive. Did he say why he took it?" Marie shook her head "Nope and as soon as they confronted him and asked him why he took it, he just shrugged noncommittally, mumbled something incoherent and walked out. Didn't even ask for a chance or anything, just left and never went back. Come on" she pleaded dramatically with her friends "you must agree that that's a bit suspicious?"

Wendy spoke first "Suspicious of doing unnatural amounts of washing maybe, but murder? That's a different kettle of fish altogether. If Barry had been killed by suffocating on washing powder, or suspicious white powder had been found under his fingernails or something I may be swaying your way, but there is still nothing to connect Darren to Barry." Her words almost echoed in the quiet room.

Steph put a finger up in the air as if testing for wind direction and wiggled it enthusiastically "Well Wend, you say there's no connection, but there is; Barry is giving us the connection." Wendy wasn't convinced "How? He could be passing through the wall into the cleaner's cupboard for any number of reasons." The others waited expectantly. "Really?" asked Marie "Name one. If he's not trying to tell us the cleaner had something to do with his untimely demise, what could he be trying to tell us? I can't think of anything else—there's nothing in there he could be leading us to, only cleaning supply's and a mop bucket—what else could he be trying to tell us?"

Wendy was struggling to come up with something else, but she gave in "Ok I can't think of anything else right now, but I won't agree to hang draw and quarter a young lad because a ghost floated through a wall and he's a bit unsociable—the lad not the ghost. We have to find something else to hang this case on." Rosie smiled cheekily at Wendy "You sound like someone off Midsummer Murders Wendy. Everyone needs to chill out a bit so we can think clearly; Steph you go and get ready to open up and I'll get the cookie's I made yesterday and make us a nice fresh cuppa to have them with".

The ladies went into motion preparing for the day; Steph went to get cash out of the safe, Marie went down to set up the till and Wendy went to unlock the door. Even though it was still five minutes till opening time, there were three people waiting outside.

It was a chilly morning so Wendy let them in a bit early. "Come on in you lot. Honestly you'll cost me my job letting you in early, but I can't let you freeze to death out there. Morning Mrs Botham, Jim and good morning to you Miss Blithe."

The two ladies said 'morning Wendy' in unison but Jim, the most unfriendly of all borrowers merely grumbled under his breath about him doing them a favour by using their shoddy library.

He pointedly looked at his watch "My watch says its nine o'clock so you should be open anyway. I pay for this library with my council tax, so the least you can bloody do on a cold grey morning is open on time to let the customers in!"

He pushed past Wendy and Mrs Botham, elbowed the door open and slammed his books on the counter. "Morning Jim, lovely to see you as always" chirped Marie, he turned mid stride to give her a death stare then carried on into the library to select his books.

Mrs Botham shook her head sadly and tutted. "Such a rude man and he used to be so nice when he worked in the garden centre. He's never been the same since they made him leave" she said quietly. Miss Blithe looked inquisitive "Why did they make him leave?" she whispered, glancing furtively to where he had disappeared into the book stacks to make sure he couldn't hear them talking about him. "Oh well, they say that the manager moved him off the cactus section, where he was perfectly happy and put him on trees and shrubs. One day a family came in looking for a fast growing conifer. He was giving them some advice, when one of the children picked a flower off one of his magnolia bushes. Apparently he had a watering can in his hand and he poured the water in it over the child whilst berating the parents for not controlling the child. It seems that it caused quite a stir and got into the local paper—although to be fair they seemed to be on his side. The garden centre manager said it was best if he retired—he was seventy eight anyway and he was always complaining about all the bending.

But he's never forgiven mankind for the garden centre siding with the family rather than him. Shame really, apparently the rest of the staff had a collection for him and bought him some lovely presents as well as making him an award for soaking the little bugger who had picked the flower." She smiled fondly at the book's she was returning and handed them to Marie "Just these two books for me sweetie thanks." She took one last look at the books she had returned and wandered off into the large print romances with Miss Blithe trailing behind her.

Rosie came back into the library with a tray of mugs and a plate of huge knobbly biscuits. "Here we go, a bit of serenity in a crazy world; tea and cookies and good company." She placed the tray carefully down on the table by the counter. Marie picked up a biscuit "What are these chunks of dark stuff?" she asked as she bit into it. Rosie pulled a secret reveal face. "Beetroot; they have sweet potato and beetroot in, it's a new recipe, what do you think?"

Steph and Wendy found they had important duties away from the counter and the offending biscuits but stayed within earshot so they could hear Marie's verdict. "Well, I think the texture is nice and there is a slightly unusual sweetness about them." She took another bite and tipped her head on one side as if she was thinking. "Mmm, now you say it, the chunks taste kind of earthy. I like them, yes definitely a good combination, pass me another" she reached over for another biscuit.

Rosie beamed with happiness "Oh I am glad you like them, Lucy said they tasted like mud and Mick wouldn't even try one". Steph and Wendy came back to the counter. Wendy picked up a biscuit hesitantly and looked at Steph. "I'm trying to watch my weight; do you want half of this one?" She said exaggeratedly. Steph looked relieved "Go on then, my trousers were a bit tight yesterday so I should definitely be cutting down on biscuits and cakes". They both bit into the biscuits tentatively and they simultaneously looked relieved, "I can see what Lucy means" said Steph "but I would say they have a nice flavour with a muddy aftertaste." she looked pleased with her assessment, but Rosie's smile faded a bit and she picked a biscuit up for herself. She bit it and looked like she was considering what everyone had said.

"I prefer earthy to muddy, but you could be right. I will definitely put this in my Baking with Vegetables book. I'll pop a couple in a bag for Matilda to take home; I know Gerald likes trying my creations".

The next couple of hours were busy in the little library. The ladies were engrossed in serving, replacing returned books and chatting to customers. They finished off their various contributions to the Anti

Addiction display and collected books for the class visit after lunch. Everyone forgot about the murder investigation for a while and stuck to the important business of being library ladies.

They locked the library up at one o'clock and retired to the staff room to eat their various packed lunches. "We need to keep an ear open, Matilda said she'd be in today and she usually surfaces just as food is exposed to the open air" Marie commented not unkindly. "Oy, stop being so mean!" Rosie elbowed Marie. "I just think lunch time is about the time her and Gerald finish their morning routine and he drops her off here so he can head off to do whatever he does in an afternoon. Nothing to do with Matilda arriving in time to eat our food." Before anyone had a chance to comment there was a knock on the back door.

Rosie gave Marie a 'you don't deserve to open the door for her' look and flounced out to let Matilda in. Marie opened her lunch box and took out a cheese salad sandwich and bit into it completely unaffected by Rosie's chastising. Matilda and Rosie came in as Steph came from the kitchen with a cup of soup and a roll. "Mmm that soup smells nice" said Matilda "is it a cuppa soup?" Steph sat down on one of the chairs. "Yes love, there's a spare one in the cupboard if you want one."

Matilda put her surprised and delighted face on "Only if you're sure Steph, I didn't realise I'd get here just as you were all eating your lunch" Matilda said innocently as she hurried into the kitchen, Marie snorted into her lunchbox, spraying masticated sandwich over her crisps.

Matilda peeped round the kitchen door with her cup of soup in her hand stirring the mixture; she looked at Marie. "Are you ok dear? You eat too fast. What you need to do is chew your food more. Oh, is that a spare sandwich?" She pointed into Marie's lunch box as Marie opened her crisps. She lifted her open lunch box up "Help yourself hun, I have crisps and a banana left anyway". She looked at Rosie who was looking intently at her own lunch. "Rosie's made some biscuits as well and put a couple in a bag for you and Gerald. Make sure you put those in your bag so you don't forget them"

Marie smiled at Matilda as she dipped the cheese sandwich in her freshly made cup of soup. Matilda looked so sweet when she was eating, so innocent and happy it made Marie feel indulgent. "I've got some Blue Ribands in my locker if you'd like one for dessert; only ninety nine calories?" Matilda looked up with a contented smile and nodded enthusiastically "Yes please, can't imagine why I'm so famished.

Must be all the housework I've done this morning" She tucked into her lunch with gusto and didn't say another word before opening time.

Wendy ate quietly but looked fed up "I told Mark I wouldn't be home for lunch today because I thought we would be discussing what happened at the meeting, but it was a bit of a let down really wasn't it?" she looked round at the others.

Rosie looked up shaking her head "Definitely not, I feel much better now we've agreed the rota for cleaning the fridge".

"That's not what I was thinking about when I decided not to go home for lunch! I thought we would have some clues or an idea if Darren was anything to do with this murder or not, but we don't do we?" She looked thoroughly dejected. Marie appreciated how she felt "Me too, a bit anyway. I don't really know what I thought would happen, perhaps that he would just spill the beans as soon as we asked him about Barry. This murder solving malachy is harder than I thought." She paused and bit into her banana. "I do think his suspicious behaviour could be a clue. We should at least put it on the crime board" she got up and started hunting round for the black marker but could only find blue chalk, so she used that to write; 'Darren—suspicious behaviour at staff meeting; warning us off getting involved'. Steph stood up to put her lunch things away "You need to be careful writing that on there. If Darren was to find that, he'd know we suspected him and he could either sue us if he's innocent and goodness knows what he could do if he's guilty" Marie pulled a face and started rubbing frantically at the chalk.

"You're right, how dumb am I?" Rosie walked past to go and open up but over her shoulder she shouted "Out of ten? Eight" and she went out laughing.

CHAPTER SEVEN

I t seemed the rest of the day was doomed for the library ladies. The class visit went well until after the discussion round up.

The children were mingling around the library looking at the books when Wendy crept up to Marie and Matilda as they were replacing books in the non fiction section. "I've just seen a lad put a book from the biology section down the front of his trousers" she whispered conspiratorially.

Marie looked furtively around "Which one—which boy was it?" There were five or six boys in the library; three with the class, a couple on their own and another lad in with his mom. "The one with dark curly hair and a hoodie" Wendy responded. "Ok, we'll split up and either confront him or if he's with the class, we'll ask the teacher to sort it." Marie said in hushed tones. They all walked stealthily in different directions to try and assess who and where the thief was.

Marie moved into the children's section surreptitiously where there were several teenage girls, a mom with a toddler and a lady on her own. As she walked round to the teenage books she spotted a dark haired lad standing on his own. He had a hoodie on so he was a possibility; she decided to get a closer look.

She walked casually up to where he was standing looking at a magazine. She pretending to be replacing some books she had picked up from the trolley and looked at the front of his trousers to see if she could spot the book.

She thought she could see evidence of it in his jeans but without her glasses, which were in the staff room, she couldn't be sure. As she looked up he was staring at her.

Caught off guard she blurted "Right young man, what's that bulge in your trousers?" pointing at the front of his jeans. The words sounded unrealistically loud and hung in the air as if time stood still.

The rest of the library was silent, well silent until Wendy walked past holding a boy with dark curly hair by his elbow and saying "You are banned young man. How could you try and steal a book that you can borrow at any time? Depriving other people of the pleasure of reading that book . . ." her voice faded as she walked into the hallway at the front of the library.

Marie felt sick as she turned back to the lad in front of her who by now was talking to his mom quietly and pointing at Marie.

A giggle came from behind Marie. "Can't wait to see your response to **that** formal complaint". Rosie obviously thought the whole thing was hilarious. Marie wanted to hurt her but she was too busy trying to think of what she could say to the boy and his mom to explain what she had said. She didn't get the chance because the boy's mom slammed the books she was holding down on the counter. She then announced in a very loud voice, "Disgusting, hardly what a mother should expect in the local library! Parents need to be warned. Come on Neil, we'll go to Northfield" and she ushered her son out of the library only stopping to look back at Marie with pure disgust on her face.

Marie sloped off to the chair by the counter and flopped into it as Wendy came back in. "Well that was easier than I thought it was going to be" she said merrily.

She looked at the others for congratulations then noticed Marie's face. She took in the way Marie was slumped in the chair and Rosie shaking with a red face standing behind her. "What's the matter love?"

Rosie stepped forward trying to suppress laughter "She stalked a young lad in the teenage section and asked him what the bulge in the front of his trousers was; she thought he was your book thief". She couldn't stop herself from laughing as she recounted the incident and as she reached the end of her sentence she was becoming hysterical. Wendy smiled and was about to join in the fun until she saw how dejected Marie looked and took pity. "Don't worry love, we can soon explain the mistake—no one would confuse you with erm the type of woman who would make sexual advances to young boys".

Rosie was uncontrollably hysterical now and tears were streaming down her face, Marie looked up at the ceiling. "Well I'm sure when his mom calls the police or the library complaints department and they come for me, I'll have plenty of time in a cell on my own to think of a credible reason for why I was pointing at a teenager boys front and asking him what the bulge was." She looked at Wendy who was trying to keep her face neutral but sympathetic, then at Rosie and suddenly began to see the funny side.

She started with a smile which migrated into a giggle then as she burst out laughing she spluttered "What the hell was I thinking?? What's that bulge in your trousers??? What sane and sober person would ever say that out loud anyway?"

She felt better now, her and Rosie kept making each other laugh, as one stopped the other one started them off again "His face" Rosie gasped "His moms face!" Marie squealed.

This went on for a few minutes so Wendy left them to it to serve people coming into and leaving the building with their books.

Steph came down the library from the office with important looking paperwork in her arms. "What's up with you two? What have I missed?" That set both of them off again and Wendy had to explain to Steph, who saw the funny side but in the back of her mind, she thought she had better note it somewhere and take a statement from Marie and the others ready for when the complaint came in. These things can go very wrong if not dealt with carefully. "Honestly Marie, how many times have I said to you to think before you speak?" Marie forced herself to stop laughing and tried to rearrange her face into a serious expression "A hundred Steph and on this occasion I genuinely wish I had. Oh well, I can't change the past no matter how hard I try so we'll just have to wait to see what his mom does."

She was calm now so sat back down to do some book repairs when the lady who lives opposite the library came in with some books to return.

"Afternoon girls and how are we all today?" she asked chirpily. Marie got up to serve her "Afternoon Mary, we're all pretty much ok, how about you?"

"I'm not too bad, still got a bit of a cold, but I'll survive. I'm a tough old bird. I noticed you all in bright and early today—thought there was trouble afoot after that nasty business with the dead body. I noticed the shutter fully up when I opened the curtains and thought to myself, that's unusual, it's usually nearly all the way down that early, but then I noticed all your cars and relaxed." She started to walk into the library to choose her books.

Marie frowned "Mary, what do you mean by 'the shutters usually nearly all the way down'?" Mary stopped and started perusing the paperback stand and said offhandedly "Well I notice that it doesn't stay fully shut down to the floor any more that's all—I presumed it had broken or something". Marie, Rosie and Steph looked at each other, minds racing.

They all gathered by the counter and called Wendy over to join them. "We shut that shutter every night all the way to the floor and when we come in in the morning, it's still shut down fully. What could

Mary mean? Wendy you know her best, can you find out what she means without alarming her? Try and get a few more details." Marie whispered. Wendy nodded and made her way over to Mary, picking up some paperbacks from the trolley to take to the paperback stand to replace. "Mary, when you say the shutter is not down to the ground, when do you mean? Is it while the library's open?" Mary stopped looking at the books for a minute and thought about the question.

"Well, when I close my living room curtains in the evening, the shutter is fully down; but when I shut my bedroom curtains as I go to bed it's up a little bit."

She nodded slightly and looked satisfied with her answer. Wendy looked back at the others for guidance and they gestured impatiently for her to carry on "Oh right, and what time do you go to bed love?" she asked nonchalantly while she put some books back on the rack. "Always the same time Wendy love, eleven o'clock. Been the same since my Tom was alive; we always headed up at eleven. Not too early, not too late he used to say, God rest him" she moved on to the next rack.

Wendy looked helplessly at the others and Steph leant forward and mouthed "Anything else different when she goes to bed?" Wendy nodded and followed Mary. "So Mary, is there anything else different when you go to bed?" Mary looked a bit puzzled "Well only that the cat used to sleep on Toms side and now he sleeps on my side. Oh and I've got a telly in the bedroom now, Tom always said we couldn't have one, but I got one after he died." Wendy smiled indulgently and said "Right, don't blame you for that, I'm sure he'd understand. I meant anything else different about the library when you go to bed." Mary looked up, as if the answer might be on the ceiling "well, there's the light. When I close the curtains in the living room there's no lights on or I cant see any anyway, but when I close the curtains in the bedroom the shutter is up a little and there is a faint light shows under it" She nodded slightly, again looked pleased with herself and moved off into the large print fiction.

Wendy joined the others by the counter. "What the hell does that mean? Who's opening the library shutter and putting a light on?" she asked conspiratorially.

Marie looked excited "It has to be Darren—he has a key. The shutter is normal by the time we get here in the morning. It has to be him, but what can he be doing here all night? Definitely not cleaning, the library's not **that** clean"

Steph put her hands up "I want to say you're jumping to conclusions again, but to be honest, I can't think of another explanation. For once, I agree, it has to be him" Wendy nodded "I agree; we have to tell the police, there may be a connection to the murder".

Marie looked crestfallen "Tell the police? Wend they're not interested; they think Barry was responsible for his own death. No we have to investigate this ourselves first to establish what is going on, if anything is going on".

The others all started talking at once "No, I definitely think we should call the police" insisted Wendy; "Are you crazy?? Investigate ourselves, a murder? A murderer?" Rosie; "I see what you're saying, what do you think we should do?" Steph nodded thoughtfully clearly up for it.

Marie put her hands up to calm everyone "Quiet! How about we stake out the library after closing to see what happens and when; if Darren comes in, we can call the police once he's inside?" Matilda appeared from the back of the library "Did I hear someone say steak?" Rosie shook her head "Not that kind of steak Matilda, the kind where you sit in the freezing cold for hours in a car outside the library waiting for a baddie to appear. I can't be staking out the library; I've got two small children to look after, and what would I tell Mick?"

"I'll do it" Steph sounded very certain "yes, I'll do it with you, we can bring a flask and snacks and hide out in one of our cars."

Marie beamed "Yes—Knew I could rely on you hun. We can go home, feed the hoards then come back here about ten o'clock to wait and see if anything happens".

The door to the library crashed open and Ashlea flew in dramatically "Well?" she said, eyebrows unnaturally high "What happened? Did he confess? What happened to my text Rosie?" Behind her Daniel, Marie's son walked in, dodging the rebound on the door. "Hey there girlies, nab your murderer yet?" he said, slightly mockingly. Marie looked impatient "No, and it's not a joking matter, this is a persons life here!" she said tersely to Daniel. "The meeting didn't give us much; just that Darren was very uncommunicative and warned us not to interfere in the police case". "Really? Well that is suspicious—Dan tell them what you told me" Ashlea urged her brother who remained unexcited.

"Oh, Daz Mann the guy who sold drugs to my mate and he ended up in hospital; well apparently he makes the drugs himself. Well, not completely, but he gets the raw ingredients and cooks them all together with random ingredients to make it go further; well he used to anyway, but his mom found out and threatened to call the police herself, so he had to stop. No one really sees him round here anymore, although he still lives with his mom. He's never there when anyone calls for him at night." Daniel finished as if his mind had already begun to wander, he picked up a magazine from the coffee table by the entrance "Ash, you gonna be long, I'm starving?" He picked up one of Rosie's biscuits, bit into it, made a face and put the rest of it back on the plate.

Ashlea looked at him as if he was a skin irritant "Well bro you can either carry on home and start cooking or wait quietly there—we have a murder to solve."

She turned back to the ladies "Well, what's the plan then? This guy must have moved his drug creation project to another location; how can we find out where he is?" The library ladies had glazed over as Ashlea was speaking. She waited a couple of seconds before saying "Hello? Earth to library ladies—what's up?" Still no one spoke or moved. Finally quietly but firmly "Here" Steph said at last "He's making his drugs here, at night." Ashlea and Daniel in unison said "Here?" they looked taken aback "How do you know?" just Ashlea this time.

"The lady that lives opposite the library said each night the shutter is down, as we leave it when we close the library, when she closes her downstairs curtains. But by the time she shuts her upstairs curtains at bedtime, the shutter is up a bit and she can see a light" Marie brought them up to speed "We had just agreed to stake out the library and if he goes in after dark, we call the police to come and catch him"

Ashlea made a whooping noise and jumped up and down on the spot. "How thrilling, what time? Shall I come here or will you pick me up?"

Marie looked at Steph who looked decidedly neutral, leaving it up to the mom "Ok, I'll pick you up, we don't want too many cars outside or he might get suspicious. Tonight just before ten although I have no idea what I'm going to tell Merch. I may just tell him the truth, he went for the whole ghost thing and didn't even blink—I think he just accepts we're all barmy".

Daniel looked up from his magazine "You should be careful with your amateur detective stuff, if Daz is the murderer, he's murdered someone."

Ashlea looked at him mystified "Profound Dan—are you coming with us then?" Daniel shook his head. "Sorry Ash, I've got football then a hot date. I don't think you should do it either, you and mom think you're Parsley and Thyme or something, but this is real and you could get into trouble" He looked genuinely worried. Ash turned away from him, no longer interested if he wasn't part of the game "Its Rosemary and Thyme you dope and if you were that worried you'd come with us. You go on your hot date and don't worry about us, we'll be fine" Daniel looked at Marie "Mom, don't do this; does Merch know what you're up to? I can't believe he'd let you stake out a potentially violent criminal. You know I would come, but I promised

Leanne we would go out tonight. I upset her on Saturday when I fell asleep in the cinema and snored all through some comedy romance she had really wanted to see. Can't you do it another night?" He was getting a bit whiney at the end; Marie patted him on his head and ruffled his hair, which he immediately moved back into place. "Don't worry son, we'll be fine, we're going to call the police the minute anything happens. There'll be no tackling him to the ground and I'll let Merch know where I am. You go off on your date".

Daniel looked appeased "Ok, if you're sure. I'm going home now, Ash I'll take the car, mom can drop you up and I'll start dinner." He kissed Marie and Ashlea and kissed Matilda on the cheek, winked at the others then disappeared out of the door.

Matilda looked dreamily after him "He's so handsome Marie, you must be very proud" Marie looked at Ashlea who was pulling a face.

"Matilda, I am proud of the work he does volunteering for Noah's Ark charity. I am proud that he's never been to prison, doesn't do hard drugs and that for most of his life has been in gainful employment. But I don't feel pride that he is handsome—that is just a freak of nature." Ashlea mumbled "I'd agree with the freak bit—you should live with him Matilda." Matilda looked even more wistful and blushed a little. "Oh it's a bit late for that kind of thing for me Ash." Ashlea made a pretend retch and shook her head "Anyway, moving swiftly on . . . What shall I bring? A torch? Sandwiches? A flask? Oh I haven't got a flask, em or a torch actually, but I could bring some crisps"

Steph smiled "I think crisps might be too noisy for a stake out. I've got hot chocolate I can bring in a flask and perhaps some biscuits.

We will have had our tea so I don't think we'll be that hungry love." Marie agreed "I think Steph's right, perhaps some quiet snacks if you have any. I'll bring grapes and chocolate buttons. I don't think we'll be hungry, but if it goes on for a few hours we will need sustenance and something to do. What about a camera to try and get photo's of him going into the library? Or if we follow him in we could snap him doing whatever he's doing."

Wendy spoke up quickly "Now hang on you lot. I only agreed not to call the police straight away because you said you'd call them if he turned up. You won't have time to take photos if you are calling the police. You just sit in the car and wait for them to arrive." She looked sternly around at them, shaking her head. "I mean it, if you don't promise to call the police straight away I'm going to call them now!" She crossed her arms to demonstrate how immovable she was being about it. Marie recognised an uncompromising stance when she saw one.

"Ok, I promise, if he turns up and goes into the library, we will call the police straight away. No need for a camera." Wendy relaxed having achieved the desired response. "Right I'll go and cash up, you lot do some replacing and start clearing people out its quarter to five." She opened the till and collected the cash and sauntered up to the office, confident she had made her point.

The others took their places on each side of the returns trolley to start putting the books in alphabetical order ready to deposit them back on the shelves. Ashlea picked up a children's book and started reading it by the counter "I'll keep an eye out in case anyone comes in".

Rosie started replacing the children's books and humming a happy tune. Steph picked up the adult non fiction in a giant pile balanced from her hand up to her shoulder "Did you mean what you said to Wendy?" she quietly asked Marie. Marie had a similar pile of adult fiction precariously resting on her wrist "Of course, I never break a promise. I didn't, however, say I would wait in the car for them to arrive" she whispered the last bit naughtily and flashed her eyes at Steph.

"I'm off now ladies, Gerald is outside and we're going to see James tonight. He's cooking us dinner and he's a very good cook so I can't wait. Sorry I can't stake out with you, but I am promised elsewhere—good luck and be careful."

She waved majestically as she left the library through the 'in' door nearly crashing into a young girl as she walked in. "Hi Jessie, we close in five minutes" Ashlea called up to the girl "Pop your books on the counter and quickly go and find one to take out" She got up and discharged the books.

Anyone watching would think she worked at the library, but it was more like she belonged there. She loved reading and was indiscriminate about what she read; taking pleasure in the act of absorbing something someone else had created. She took after her mom that way; they would both read anything and loved being surrounded by books. She discharged Jessie's books and popped them on the trolley, then sat down, tucked her legs up onto the chair and went back to the children's book she had picked up.

Five minutes later, Jessie had gone with a new selection of hastily chosen books in hand, leaving with the other people still in the library at five o'clock. Rosie locked up behind them and came back into the library with an exaggerated sigh. "Well that's Monday over with—apart from the bit where I wrestle with two over tired children, force feed them food they don't want thanks to the rubbish they will have consumed all day, chat banally with a husband who isn't interested in what I have to say and generally spend the evening unappreciated until I fall into bed feeling sorry for myself and looking forward to coming to work, when my life calms down considerably!" Steph grinned at her "You just described my life if you transpose the over tired children with over opinionated teenagers! Those people who say mothers should stay at home and look after their children full time clearly don't have any of their own. If I didn't come to work I would more than likely turn to drink to keep me numb or drink myself to oblivion daily to rescue myself from the devilish reality I have created."

Wendy looked affronted; she pulled her cardigan round her and hugged it to demonstrate her disapproval. "Mothers should be at home with their children, it's our nature, our duty.

I would definitely have stayed home with mine if we could have afforded it—actually I still would if I could and they're in their thirty's and don't live with me any more!" she laughed at herself.

They all started walking down the library towards the staff room "It could all be over tonight" Marie said sombrely "We may find out who killed poor Barry and he can really rest in peace". "If we do, we should hold a special kind of service for him in the library, you know to say goodbye and that." Rosie suggested "Aah that sounds nice, can your sister do it for us cos she's a proper vicar" asked Ashlea "Minister. I'll ask her" said Rosie "if she cant I'll get her to email us something appropriate we can say and we'll do it ourselves".

Steph held the door open for the others, "Problem is if we solve Barry's murder mystery by finding it was Darren; it's another life over—Darren's. He's only in his twenty's and he will go to prison. Plus it must be tormenting him, don't you think? Knowing what he's done?" A rare quiet moment followed, the enormity of the impact of their proposals had made them all thoughtful.

"If he has any conscience at all it should be tormenting him whether he goes to prison or not, if he did it. We can't be worrying about Darren, we have to concentrate on getting justice for Barry. He's the innocent victim here, not Darren." Said Rosie indignantly.

"I know, but it's just that with every life taken by murder, there's at least another one ruined because of the crime. I'm not saying it's not fair, I'm just saying it's sad because after tonight, it could be his life over as well" Steph said poignantly.

Everyone went quiet, a heavy oppressive silence starting to engulf them. They collected their coats, bags and other oddments and stood without speaking waiting for Wendy to finish cashing up and come to collect her things.

The door opened and Wendy charged into the room oblivious to the atmosphere. "I must remember to stop for toilet rolls on the way home; poor Mark said he had to use kitchen roll lunchtime which meant an embarrassing dash down to the kitchen apparently, cos he didn't notice until he had done the deed. Still, he could have gone out and bought some instead of texting me to! Typical bloke." She opened her locker "Right ho our gang, time for home, reality awaits." She looked round at the others puzzled when they didn't respond. "What's up with you lot? Why're you so quiet?" Marie spoke broodingly on behalf of the others. "I think the reality of what could happen tonight has made us all think about the gravity of the situation. Barry lost his life and if Darren is guilty of his murder, he has ruined his and we've been treating it all like a bit of a game. But it's not a game, its serious; dead serious." Wendy's face softened as she looked at Marie. "Hun, it doesn't matter how you have treated this whole thing. You haven't done anything wrong. So what if we've all let ourselves play Miss Marple, we didn't do anything criminal. Barry's ghost called to us in desperation and we answered that call. We found his lifeless rotting body tossed in the undergrowth like unwanted leftover meat.

If we discover that Darren killed Barry and he ends up in prison and with the stigma of that with him forever, we didn't do that to Darren, he did it to himself. If he gets away with it, he might do it again—now that would be something we'd have a right to feel guilty about! If we had our suspicions and we did nothing; that would be wrong. The police have given up on Barry, but we haven't—we have nothing to feel guilty about. All that said; don't forget you promised you would call the police if he does turn up at the library. Now come on you lot, chin up—off home to prepare for your stake out" looking at Marie, Steph then Ashlea "or domestic bliss" eyebrows raised looking at Rosie, who laughed "or dirty bum rescue" pointing at herself "I for one have had enough for one day!"

She ushered them all out of the staff room and stepped back to switch off the light. As she turned to follow the others out, in the dark, she felt a gentle breeze on her face that sent a shiver down her spine. She stopped for a second as if she was expecting something else to happen, but nothing did, so she mentally shrugged and walked out of the room.

Wendy didn't get straight into her car. She walked over the road and into the Tesco supermarket to get some toilet rolls. She picked up a basket and started wandering round the shop. She wasn't really concentrating, she was thinking about Barry and wondering what had actually happened to him; was he an innocent victim, or the burglar the police thought he was. Was he involved in something sinister that ended up costing him his life, or was he oblivious to what was going to happen to cut his life so short?

Bumping into a display of chocolate fingers brought her thoughts back to the shop, and as she picked up the few that she had knocked over, she popped a couple in her basket—buy one get one free—cant go wrong.

Rosie drove to the childminder and became cross with the world when she got there, only to be told that Mick had already picked the children up. She couldn't remember if he had told her he was going to get them, so she didn't know whether she could be mad at him or not. That's the problem when you're responsible for small children; their schedule of activities, a job and a busy husband. Your mind turns to slush and forgets to sort out the important information from the ordinary crap.

She was in a foul mood by the time she arrived home fifteen minutes later. She slammed the car door to pay back the car for being witness to her wasted journey, stamped up the steps to her house and viciously dug in her bag for her door keys, not caring that she was behaving like a petulant child. The door opened before she found her keys and Mick was standing in front of her in an apron. He greeted her with a beaming smile that lit up his face, "About time you got here, me and the kids have prepared a special dinner for you madam. Follow me." He bowed majestically.

He marched Rosie into the dining room where the two children stood up straight with aprons made out of bath towels and tea towels folded over their arms. "Madam" they both said and bowed awkwardly. Mick pulled back a chair and waved her into it, she still hadn't said a word—couldn't actually think of one to say. The table was set out formally with cutlery laid out, dinner plates, side plates, bowls and glasses; she smiled serenely as Mick opened a bottle of wine and started pouring it into her glass.

"I don't know what to say" she said rather overwhelmed; she could feel tears forming in her eyes. Mick kissed her head "You don't have to say anything princess, we don't tell you how much we appreciate you enough, so tonight is your night. Spaghetti bolognaise made with non meat mince, followed by Eaton mess. It was going to be meringue nests but Billie dropped the box of meringues." Billie pulled a face and Lucy gave him a look and a shove. Rosie laughed and winked at Billie "Eaton mess, my favourite. I prefer them mashed up anyway, so thanks for that Billie" Billie smiled and wrinkled up his nose at Lucy. "How perfect this all is. I was in a rotten mood when I walked up those stairs and ready to shout or moan or just sulk and you, my lovely family, you have blown it away like a cloud. Thank you." She controlled her wobbly voice and smiled widely at them all in turn "Right then, where's the food, I'm starving!"

Steph's house resembled Blackpool illuminations again when she got home. She could see all the lights burning electricity from the bottom of the small cul de sac they lived in. Bloody kids, bloody men do they think it's free? Steph was winding herself up as she drove up the road and parked in front of the house. Is it too much trouble to remember to turn a light off as you leave a room? She asked herself posing the question to her family in her head. She was ready to call them all in a room and show them the electricity bill and in turn ask them how they would pay for it. That would make them think. She organised all the bills and consequently everyone apparently thought everything was free. She put her key in the door, cursing the ugly looking board still covering the broken door window. She entered the modern house hesitantly, and hung her coat up in the bright spacious hall listening for where the family were.

Eugenie was in her room, she knew this because Eugenie was the only one of their daughters who liked rock music and rock music was playing upstairs. The other two hated it. It wasn't too loud though, so no need to intervene. She mentally ticked off her list containing four members, down to three. Nigel was in the lounge, she could see his feet crossed over on the carpet so she popped her head round the door. "Hi honey I'm home" she smiled; no response—Nigel was fast asleep in his chair and Gilly was on the settee with her headphones on and eyes shut listening to music. Two more off the list and actually it didn't matter too much where Bella was because she was the most sensible of them all (including Nigel) and she was clearly not in any sort of conflict with either of her sisters. Steph decided to start on the dinner and get everyone fed and settled (some chance) so that she could head off for her spot of detective work knowing she had carried out her motherly / wifely duties first.

If she played her cards right, she could sneak out without anyone knowing. Nigel would eat his dinner and fall back to sleep and the girls would scatter to the four, well three of the four corners of the house as soon as they had eaten. This would give Steph ample opportunity to change in to dark clothing, an essential she felt for the stake out, and then grab some snacks and depart. She was quite excited. She had a niggle of fear just in case Darren did turn up but she had an equal amount of tickle that was anticipation for exactly the same reason.

She looked in the freezer and considered what to cook; something simple so she could dream about the adventures ahead—aah pizza, wedges and salad, no real need for input she could just pop them in the oven, tip the salad onto plates, set the oven timer and dream away, perfect!

Marie pulled up outside Ashlea's house. "Right hun, I'll be back for you about five to ten. Make sure you wrap up warm cos we'll have to turn the engine off so the car will get cold. In fact, bring your furry blanket." She leaned over to kiss Ashlea before she got out of the car. "Ok mom, ooh I can't wait it feels like we are about to solve the crime of the century! Do you think we might actually catch Daz in the act? Cooking up designer drugs?" She picked up her bag and started rooting around for her keys.

"I don't honestly know love, I don't actually know what designer drugs are, but I do think the pieces of this puzzle are starting to fall into place and tonight we may just find out what happened to Barry. Now get inside and make sure you have something filling for your tea. See you later." Ashlea got out of the car and skipped up her path turning for a quick wave before she went through the door.

Marie turned the car around and became aware of the song playing on the radio; Watching the Detective by Elvis Costello, she smiled at how appropriate it was. She drove home in a bit of a dream, thinking about the day and wondering how the night would play itself out.

She pulled up on her drive a few minutes later, the house looked cosy and inviting with the curtains closed and the lights on; Merch must be home. She locked the car and started walking up to the door as it opened "Oh babs, I thought I heard you, have you brought bread? We've run out and I fancy cheese on toast for tea" He walked ahead of her into the kitchen to make a cup of tea for them both. Marie looked at his back, he never had the slightest interest in her day and never asked about it, she often wondered about this.

Could it be that he was only concerned with their joint life and anything outside that didn't involve him was unimportant? She puzzled over it many times, but they were so happy and well matched it seemed too small an issue to ever bring up. "We have bread in the bread bin. Are you sure you only want toast? I was going to do you steak and rice". He turned round with an endearing smile on his handsome face, "Oh, lovely, steak and rice then, but I have to pop out for a bit later, going to help your John with his car" he passed Marie her tea, John was her brother and never had money for a mechanic so he and

Merch spent hours tinkering with one problem or another on his cars. "Well I have to go out as well, we think our cleaner is connected to the dead body we found and someone said the library shutter is being opened after we've gone home so we're going to stake out the library tonight for a couple for hours."

Even to Marie, who knew what she was talking about, that sounded confusing but Merch just looked at her, "What time are you going out then?" Marie opened the fridge to get the steak out "Around half nine and we'll probably be a couple of hours" Merch didn't look very impressed "We?", "Me, Ash and Steph." Merch looked exasperated "How did Ashlea get dragged into this? You and Steph are barking with your ghost stories and murderers on the loose, but Ashlea? You'd think she'd have something more interesting to do with her evening at her age" He shook his head and went out of the kitchen without waiting for an answer.

Marie got on with dinner and didn't think any more about the discussion or Merch's reaction. She was planning what outfit to change into and deciding which warm blanket and snacks to take.

Matilda was in her element at James's house. She spent the evening playing with her beautiful granddaughter, who at four was perfect company for Matilda. She sat on her lap and listened to her stories cuddled up in her grandma's arms until eventually she fell asleep and her mother retrieved her to take her up to bed. "Tonight some of the girls are staking out the library to see if the murderer is our cleaner." She announced to Gerald and James who were both watching the news. "Really mom, how very brave of them" said James, his eyes never leaving the screen. Gerald didn't comment, it is possible he didn't hear Matilda. A couple of minutes later James frowned and looked at his mom "Did you say some of the other library ladies are staking out the library to see if a murderer turns up there?" He sounded decidedly uncertain.

"Yes James, we have uncovered some clues that have led us to believe that the cleaner could be using the library for illegal purposes. It is too much of a stretch of the imagination to believe that it isn't connected to Barry's body being discovered—West Heath library is hardly a hotbed of criminal activity." Matilda explained carefully. James patted his dads arm, "Dad, did you hear mom? Is it true? Those women are taking an awful risk if the guy is a criminal. Who knows what a desperate man will do if he thinks a clutch of nosey women are about to trap him doing something illegal. They should keep well out of it and call the police!" James was plainly worried by his mother's revelation but Gerald just shook his head resignedly. "Son if there is one thing I have learned from years of being married to your mom it is that women make no sense at all and won't do anything you tell them. No point telling these girls that they shouldn't be doing a stake out because that will make them all the more determined. Anyway, the whole story sounds like nonsense to me; a cleaner making drugs at the library? Preposterous."

He turned back to the television the subject obviously closed. James still looked dissatisfied and it looked as if he was about to continue when his wife, Juliet poked her head round the living room door. "James, Jemima wants you to read her a story. Can you go up to her and I will make hot chocolate for everyone?" She smiled, but it was obviously not really a question. James smiled at his wife and got up "Ok sweetheart" he turned to his parents, "won't be long". He ambled up the stairs, all thoughts of worry about the library ladies gone. Matilda picked up Juliet's magazine and immediately became engrossed in a short story about a dog that could speak to its owner.

CHAPTER EIGHT

Marie text Steph 'Meet at 10pm in Tesco car park. Park at the back where the staff cars are. Got chocolate and cheese biscuits'. Steph text back 'ok. Got flask and choc buttons and blanket x'. Marie text Ashlea 'Pick you up at 5 2 10. Bring blanket x'. Ashlea text Marie 'K got crisps (puffs so quiet) ☺ x'. Rosie text Marie and Steph 'Be careful. Good luck. X'.

CHAPTER NINE

Marie collected her stake out kit to take out to the car. It consisted of a pack of six milky ways, six packets of cheese thins, a fleece blanket, a pack of tissues (you just never know) and a torch. She pulled her warm coat with a furry hood down off the coat rack and slipped it on as she contemplated the possibilities of the evening ahead.

She had actually exhausted all the connotations of what she could imagine would happen while she was making tea for Merch and afterwards soaking in the bath. She had been too excited to eat much so stuck with cheese on toast and an aero. Merch had already been gone for an hour giving Marie plenty of time to do nothing whatsoever in preparation for the stake out, apart from sort out the chocolate and snacks. She didn't even have to sort out the fleece blanket because it was the one her and Merch kept behind the settee to pull over themselves when they were laying watching telly.

She had to admit to being very excited and equally afraid. In her imaginings Darren was much bigger and the police took too long to get to them and he spotted them and had a gang with him. Marie had to stop her wild imagination or she would frighten herself out of going through with it! She walked back into the kitchen to get her car keys and caught sight of her own reflection. Did she see an amateur sleuth off to solve her first crime or a ridiculous middle aged woman with too much time on her hands and a vivid imagination? Actually she saw her mascara had run so that distracted her while she wiped it off and broke the reflective moment. She picked her keys and stake out kit up and headed for the door.

Ashlea was waiting by the door when Marie pulled up outside her house. She ran up her path nearly tripping herself up with her blanket, which was already draped over her shoulders. She opened the door beaming from ear to ear "I am so excited, I have been waiting outside for ten minutes! Everyone thinks I'm bonkers but I don't care—Nothing this adventurous has ever happened to me before.

I brought wotsits instead of crisps because I thought we could suck them and they dissolve". She buckled up her seatbelt and took the first breath since she had launched into the car.

Marie smiled in the dark. Pride is a funny thing, you can be proud of your children's achievements, proud of their actions and proud of yourself for your parenting skills. But the unexpected swell you get in your chest for the most irrational things like seeing them happy or excited about something doesn't really have a word for it—pride isn't it but it will have to do or maybe it was just love.

They drove quietly up to the supermarket. It was only a five minute walk away but they had to go in the car or they wouldn't be properly staking the joint out and three ladies hanging about in the dark was hardly inconspicuous. So they drove into the car park and parked in the corner where you wouldn't see the car from the library.

"Shouldn't we be able to see the library door to stake it out?" Ashlea asked reasonably. "We will move when Steph gets here. We only want to use one car don't we, so one of us can leave our car here and the other one can drive down a bit closer." Marie responded just as Stephs car headlights illuminated the inside of her car. Marie got out of the car and Ashlea followed. They went over to Steph. "Whose car shall we survey from do you think? Mine is darker but it's only got two doors so a quick exit from the back is out. Yours is probably a bit more noticeable than mine though because you've had it longer and Darren is more likely to have seen it outside the library. What do you think?" Marie said in a hushed voice.

Steph looked a bit startled already "I think your car then. Nigel would go mad if anything happened to this car and at least Merch can repair yours if anything goes down" she said. Marie screwed up her face "What on earth do you think could 'go down' that would damage the car?" Steph shrugged "Who knows? Whatever, I don't want it to happen to my car so lets go in yours." She got out of her car and walked to Marie's and got in the passenger seat, leaving a completely flabbergasted Marie standing by Stephs car. Marie shook her head and nodded to Ashlea to go back to her car. They both got in, Ashlea in the back and Marie reversed the car out of the car park. "Lights might help" Steph said hands gripping her seat, a trace of panic in her voice as Marie drove slowly down the road outside the library with no lights on. "Don't be soft! We don't want anyone to notice us. I'll pick out space on the opposite side of the road. Pity we don't know which way he will be coming so we can be facing him ready to duck down so he doesn't spot us." Marie carried on regardless. "One of us will have to keep watch out the back window and one forwards and one covering both" said Ashlea strategically as they pulled up at the side of the road directly opposite the alley beside the library. They all looked up the alley remembering the last time they spent any time down there. "Poor Barry" mumbled Steph. The other two nodded solemnly.

They sat quietly for a couple of minutes before Ashlea was unable to keep from speaking "Shall we have something to eat? This stake out business is making me hungry". She peeped in the bag her mom had brought and picked out a packet of cheesy biscuits and contentedly started munching them. Marie smiled indulgently in the rear view mirror and Steph shook her head "Ash, we've only been here ten minutes, you can't be hungry yet. We've hardly settled in to the stake out".

Ashlea looked up from her biscuits at Steph "Steph, its not just the time we've been here. The whole evening has been building up to this moment, I feel like I am on an important mission, like we could crack this whole case wide open tonight and its making me hungry! I do think it's important that we keep our energy levels up too, we could be here for hours." she said dramatically and reasonably at the same time. "Well not really hun, Mary said the shutters are already partially up by the time she goes to bed at eleven. Its twenty five to eleven now, so if it's going to happen it will be within the next twenty to twenty five minutes." Marie pointed out sensibly. Ashlea tilted her head on one side and swallowed "Well, we should definitely eat the stuff then or we won't have time." Steph and Marie smiled at each other and Steph passed her and Ashlea a packet of chocolate buttons "Fair point, here you go".

They all sat quietly eating; Ashlea was sitting sideward with her feet up on the back seat so that she could look out the back of the car up the road and Marie and Steph were watching the front. Steph broke the silence "What did you tell Merch? Where does he think you are?" Marie shrugged "Here. I told him I was here and that we were staking out the library for the possible murderer of Barry. The only thing he thought was odd was that Ash was here and not off doing something more interesting for a young person." She pulled a fed up face. Ashlea gasped loudly "What?? More interesting than this? He doesn't know what he's saying how can anything be more exciting than staking out a murderer?" Ashlea couldn't believe her ears.

Steph shook her head aghast "So he didn't mind you being here then. I had to sneak out, I just fed them all and off they went to their rooms, Nigel was asleep before I had finished washing up.

I just showered, found my dark jumper and jeans and came out, if any of them notice I'm missing they will call or text me. My phone's on silent. Sod em." She smiled and fished her flask out of the carrier bag by her feet. She passed out cups to Marie and Ashlea and started pouring hot chocolate out for them all. They all settled back contented. Two sips into her drink Marie saw a shape moving slowly up the road, keeping close to the building line and looking around. "Is that him?" she whispered pointing at the figure.

It was hard to distinguish in the dark, the lamp post was out and the figure kept to the shadows. Steph sucked in her breath through pursed lips "Yes, that's him and he's coming towards us so duck down". Ashlea climbed onto the floor "oops, sorry mom I've spilt chocolate on the seat" she whispered huskily. Marie flapped her hand trying to get the top of her body out of sight of the outside world and the approaching Darren "Don't worry about that now!" she slipped most of her body under the steering wheel keeping the top of her head just high enough so she could see Darren as he walked towards the library on the opposite side of the road.

Steph was completely in the foot well of the passenger side hugging her cup "Is he here? Is he going to the library? What can you see?" Marie hand flapped again "Shhh will you, I will let you know when he gets here. He's stopped by the alley." She said so quietly the other two could only just hear her. "He's going up the steps and he's got a dark army type bag in his hand" Marie updated softly. She twisted her body round a bit because her legs were going to sleep, "he's opening the shutter, the little sodbag, it is him. Ok, he's going in the door—oh" she ducked down as far as she could "He's looking over here" She stayed very still.

The three of them stopped breathing they were so still; if they could have stopped the loud thumping of their hearts, they would have. They waited a minute, then Marie peered over the steering wheel. "He's in and I can see his hand pulling the shutter down manually from inside. That's why it's up a bit when he's inside, he has to pull his hand back in and so he leaves a little gap. He'd need that to push it back up again from inside too."

She started extracting herself stiffly from under the steering wheel, "Christ, three minutes wedged down there and I feel like I've been in a car accident." She started rubbing her legs vigorously. "Come on you two, what're you doing?" Neither Steph nor Ashlea had made a move to leave their hiding places. Steph groaned and put her hand up towards Marie "Ooh I'm not sure I can get myself out. Give us a pull will you?" Marie pulled her hand and then arm and Steph managed to get up onto the seat, landing with a loud huff. Ashlea had climbed up onto the back seat while this had been going on. "Well what's our next move then mom?" she asked animatedly leaning into the space between the two front seats.

Steph looked expectantly at Marie "You promised Wendy you would phone the police as soon as Darren got here" she said. Marie put her hand up as if to stop Steph "And I will, but perhaps not straight away. If we call them now he won't have had a chance to do anything will he? How about we finish our snacks, go out to stretch our legs, then phone the police?" She said reasonably. Steph seemed about to comply but Ash got in first "Definitely a good plan. Only one flaw—I think we should go in the library before the police get here to see if we can get him to admit to killing Barry". She got her wotsits out and passed them round.

Marie looked at Steph to try and gauge her reaction to Ashlea's suggestion. She was clearly considering the proposal seriously, "I suppose Ash has a point. If the police get here and don't believe he had anything to do with the murder, they might get him for the drugs—if that's what he's doing, but not bother to investigate Barry. That would be a travesty wouldn't it?" Steph looked at Marie and Ashlea who were nodding enthusiastically.

Marie spoke "You're right Steph, it's practically our duty to try and sort the murder out, after all Barry himself put us in charge. Right we're agreed then" she said decisively "we'll wait a bit longer then phone the police before heading in there ourselves." Just saying it out loud gave Marie nervous butterflies in her stomach.

CHAPTER TEN

They all sat quietly absorbing the words for a minute. Suddenly lights shone in front of them as a car pulled up just down from the library. "Oh shit, someone else is there—I never thought about him having an accomplice" Marie said in a panic. "Duck down—it could be a gang." Steph shot down into the foot well again and Ashlea lay flat across the back seats while Marie slid her body onto the floor under the steering wheel. They all stayed perfectly still, straining to hear any noise outside; there was the sound of a door slamming. Ashlea made a squeaking noise and they all squeezed themselves even smaller. Marie started to lift her head up inch by inch "I'm going to have to have a look, see if they have gone into the library" she peeped over the steering wheel. "I can't see anyone—whaaaaaaaaa" They all screamed as a bang on the window scared them half to death.

The door opened and Rosie stuck her head in "What are you lot doing hiding down there? You'll never see anything if you don't actually look through the windows" She was laughing.

"You idiot! You could have given us all a heart attack—we thought you were Darren's gang." Marie wasn't laughing, but at least she was relieved it wasn't a gang. Rosie sniggered. "What, all by myself? What kind of a gang pulls up in a people carrier?"

Steph spoke for the first time "Well to be fair Rosie it looked like a big gangsta car from here in the dark. You can't imagine how scary this stake out has been." Ashlea looked questioningly at Steph "Really? Have we been on the same one?" A noise distracted them all at the same time; it was another car coming down the road. "Get down Rosie" whisper shouted Marie urgently. "There's another car". Rosie knelt down on the curb, ducking her head inside the driver's side by Marie who had slipped onto the floor again. The car coming down the road stopped right outside the library. It was a black or dark coloured saloon style but they couldn't see who was in it because the windows were tinted, adding to the ominous look of the vehicle to the hiding ladies.

They all stooped down so the occupants of the car couldn't see them. They heard a door open and held their breath. "Thank you" rang out Matilda's voice. The ladies all popped their heads up at the same time like a bunch of Meer cats in time to see Matilda waving to them dressed in a full length pink quilted housecoat with a green woollen hat and scarf and slippers.

"Whooee, girls it's me, Matilda" she called as she walked across the road to where they were all now standing in clear view, astounded. Snapping back to life Rosie dashed across to Matilda, grabbed her elbow and shushed her whilst pulling her across to the others. She went round to the driver's side and pulled Marie out unceremoniously and sat Matilda down side wards on the driver's seat. "Now Matilda first of all what are you doing here and secondly be quiet! This is supposed to be a stake out so we need to maintain a low profile" Rosie whispered insistently. "Actually we have not maintained a low profile since you turned up and while we're on the subject, what are you doing here?" Marie asked Rosie. "I couldn't sleep thinking about you lot here. Everyone else was asleep but I just couldn't drop off no matter how many cats I counted. All I kept thinking was if something happened to any of you and I wasn't here I would never forgive myself. Also I thought of how exciting it was and I was missing out on the fun, so I just left a note in the kitchen in case Mick woke up, grabbed my car keys and hit the road. What about you Matilda?"

"Almost the same really. Gerald had fallen asleep reading his paper as usual after we got back from James and Juliet's and I went upstairs to get ready for bed. As I was brushing my hair I had a vision in my head of you lot all dressed in black congregating outside the library holding onto Darren with Barry floating in front of you and I thought, no I need to be part of this, Barry needs me" she nodded a very sincere face. Marie put a hand on her arm "Matilda, can you get to the bit where you decided to come in your nightclothes? If anyone sees you in that there going to think you're a ghost. You couldn't be brighter if you had a high viz jacket on!"

"Oh I called a taxi from the bedroom and went straight out to it when it came. Problem was I left my coat and boots in the dinning room and if I had gone through the lounge, where Gerald was asleep, to fetch them, he might have woken up and there was no way he would let me out at this time of night, especially in my night clothes." Marie smiled confusedly "He may have had a valid point" she said quietly.

"Well we can't stay here now, there are too many of us to fit in the car. We're going to have to go in." She leaned into the car and said to Ashlea and Steph "Come on you two, time for action". Steph got out of the car and held the seat forward for Ashlea to climb out. Steph came round to the drivers side "Marie" she whispered urgently and indicated for Marie to move slightly away from the others with her. Thinking she had an idea Marie followed her willingly and leaned her head down to hear what she had to say. "Sorry but when Rosie banged on the window I wee'd in your car." She mumbled. Marie looked at her in astonishment "Honestly Steph? Bloody hell, with your wee and Ashlea's hot chocolate, no wonder you didn't want to use your bloody car". She sighed and walked back up to the others dolefully shaking her head.

Ashlea looked at her puzzled as if she was going to ask what was up, but Marie put her hand up to stop any questions. "Well, we need to split up; we can't all go charging over there at once, the neighbours will think there's a riot! How about me Steph and Ash go first? We'll pull the shutter up manually as slowly and quietly as possible, we'll unlock the door, climb in and if the coast is clear You and Matilda come over. Wait in the car out of sight until I give you a signal." she said to Rosie, who nodded.

She looked at Ashlea and Steph (who was still looking a bit sheepish); they both nodded and seemed to rise up a bit with importance filling out their chests. Marie started walking up the path on the same side of the road as the car heading towards Tesco, Matilda called out "Are you going to the shop first Marie? I could do with some chocolate." Marie turned round with a face like thunder and stomped back down to the car. Everyone shrunk back a bit, "I am walking up this way so that we can cross the road up by the shop and NOT directly in front of the library. We will be circling back on ourselves so that anyone seeing us won't guess we are going into the library. We'll keep to the shadows sneaking up the steps and trying to stay out of site because unlike you, I realise how important it is to remain inconspicuous!" "Well you won't remain very inconspicuous if you keep shouting" Matilda said completely unaffected by Marie's wrath. Marie grunted and started walking determinedly up the dark road towards the supermarket, followed closely by Ashlea and Steph. As she reached the entrance to the car park she stopped, looked around and crossed over the road, again the other two followed a few steps behind. They met up outside the old cottage built long before anything else on the road and next to the alley by the side of the library. They huddled under a large laurel bush to give instructions to each other. "I'll creep up now and start work on the shutter" Marie whispered. Steph shook her head, "You won't be able to do that quietly by yourself. You'll need hands all the way along so it doesn't squeal. We'll all have to do it".

They all looked at each other and by silent mutual agreement they crept along the garden wall, dodging an overgrown rose bush and slipped into the alley. They stealthily made their way one at a time across the alley and up the steps in front of the library crouching down in front of the shutter.

Marie did fingers on lips gesture to the others and pointed to Ashlea then the end of the shutter and then at Steph and the middle of the shutter. They all grabbed the bottom of the metal shutter and Marie nodded. They moved the shutter up one inch at a time, each groan sounding like a clap of thunder to their frightened ears. It felt like forever to get the shutter up and they were petrified that everyone in West Heath could hear the clanging and squeaking of the old metal contraption. No one appeared; not even a face in a window or a curtain twitch. When they had it half way up, the keyhole in the door was showing so they stopped.

Marie pulled a face and whispered "Damn, we didn't phone the bloody police. Ash, text Rosie to phone them now, but make sure your phone is on silent in case she replies". They stood slightly away from the door as Ashlea text Rosie as instructed. They all shivered; not only was it absolutely freezing, but the night was so silent it was eerie and combined with the trepidation about what might happen, they all had the creeps. By now it was close to midnight and they were all feeling tired but alert and buzzing with adrenalin. It was a bit like trying to sleep when you've had too much caffeine.

Marie took the key out of her pocket and slid it carefully into the keyhole. The scraping noise as the key went in sounded like chalk on a blackboard to their sensitive frightened ears, the click as it unlocked sounded like a drum roll. They waited, holding their breath to see if any of the din they made alerted Darren. Each time the silence remained unbroken inside the library. Marie grasped the handle of the door firmly and gently and slowly pressed it down and pushed the door forward. They all crouched down and waited, ready to bolt if they heard movement inside. Nothing.

Marie looked over her shoulder at the others and solemnly nodded her head. She started to gently move herself into the library through the slightly opened door. She looked like a drunk in slow motion on all fours trying to remain hidden as she slipped through the door. Ashlea was next, determined not to leave her mom alone in the library for long she squatted low and climbed in sidewards not making a sound. Steph bent over and clambered through the gap in an ungainly leap. They all stayed low in the dark and quiet. They waited again to see if they had alerted Darren to their presence, but still nothing stirred inside the library. Marie put her finger on her lips again to indicate shush to the others and quietly went back to the library door.

She popped her head through the bottom half of the open door and looked over to where Rosie and Matilda were waiting for their signal. Marie waved for them to come over. She stayed watching to make sure they had seen her. She saw Rosie get out of the car on the opposite side of the car and gesture thumbs up. She was followed by Matilda who slammed the car door shut behind her. Marie rolled her eyes and gritted her teeth in the dark because the noise seemed so loud she was beginning to think Darren must have something wrong with his hearing not to hear the commotion outside the library at nearly bloody midnight!

They walked furtively up the road, taking the same path as Marie, Steph and Rosie had earlier. Marie lost sight of them as they went far enough up to cross over out of sight of the library. She waited a minute, looking at the spot where they would emerge the other side of the library alley. She waited more, getting a little concerned at how long it was taking them to get round to the library. She looked at the other two behind her; she shrugged her shoulders and shook her head.

Worried now that something had happened to the ladies she gesticulated that she was going back out to look and the girls should stay put. She crawled back out of the slightly opened door and under the half up shutter and tiptoed down the steps. As she rounded the corner she saw that Rosie was trying to unhook Matilda from a rose bush in the front garden of the cottage next door. Marie's eyes widened in astonishment—Matilda was a liability! She went up to the other two and frustrated she whispered through gritted teeth. "How the hell did you get stuck on this?" As she helped to pick Matilda's quilted housecoat off the bush leaving bits of quilted inner fluff on the thorns. "I thought I heard something so I jumped closer to the garden and got stuck in this bush" Matilda whispered defensively back. Marie signed heavily and pulled the last bit of housecoat off the bush. She looked at Rosie who signalled that she was helpless to prevent the incident. "Come on, I've had to leave the other two on their own with a dangerous criminal in there to come and find you two numpties!"

She started walking determinedly towards the library, then remembered she was supposed to be staying out of sight and shiftily slid into the alley then stooped to climb up the steps. She gestured for the other two to follow. She let Rosie go into the library then moved back for Matilda who looked a bit hesitant. "I don't think I can fit through that gap" she whispered. Marie looked as if she might scream and blow the whole thing, but instead she leaned in and pushed the door, very slowly open another few inches. She raised her eyebrows at Matilda to enquire if that was ok. Matilda screwed her face up, but crouched down never the less. She got onto all fours and started clambering through the open door; unfortunately her housecoat got snagged on the shutter and pulled it creating a loud groaning noise which stopped her dead in her tracks. They all stayed perfectly still, not moving, not breathing. They heard nothing.

After a minute or so a very sweaty Marie carefully unhooked Matilda and tapped her to carry on in. Eventually Marie climbed back in and pushed the door until it was almost closed.

They all stood up and looked at Marie. She realised that she hadn't really thought this through; she had no idea what to do next. Quickly she evaluated what they wanted—what was their desired outcome? They wanted to catch Darren in the act of cooking up drugs and then get him to confess to Barry's murder. When she thought it out like that it seemed ridiculous. She had managed to get almost the complete library staff and her own daughter into the library with a criminal, a probable murderer at midnight with no forward planning what so ever. Great strategy.

She mouthed her words now with very little actual sound "Right, we need to get Darren out of the staff room into the library in case he has any weapons in there" Ashlea and Matilda nodded, Steph went white and Rosie gulped. "We need a volunteer to go into the office, lock the office door to the main library behind them then wait for us to tempt Darren out before dashing into the staff room and locking it from the inside so he cant get back in". She looked around at the others, Matilda spoke up "I'll do it" she said bravely. Marie looked at the others, eyes wide as if to prompt a more appropriate volunteer—no luck. "Steph, I was thinking you might be good at this. Matilda I'm a bit worried about you getting your dressing gown stuck somewhere and Darren getting back in to you." Matilda caught Marie's eye and leaned forward to whisper "It's a housecoat dear".

Steph put her hand out to attract attention. "Ok, I'll do it. I've got the keys here" She patted a small bag which she had across her body and blew out a puff of air as if to calm herself. Marie smiled at her, "Right, you and I will be the only ones he sees. Ash and Rosie you hide in the non fiction somewhere he won't be able to see you. Matilda, you go into the children's area, that way you can have a sit down and there will be no danger of you tripping over anything or catching your dres em housecoat on anything and making a noise." Marie took a deep breath and pushed her (considerable) chest out—fully in charge now. "We need to take very careful quiet steps slowly into the library, one step then a gap, then another step and so on, in case he hears one of the footsteps. If it's quiet after each step, hopefully if he does hear anything he will just think it's the library creaking. Me and Steph will go first, but the rest of you follow putting your feet down at the same time as we do. Don't come too far into the library before you find your hiding place; if he comes out and runs into the stacks I don't want him finding one of you." She looked at each of them in turn, as if they were going into battle. "Right lets do this."

She held out her hand to Steph and they took the first step together, like you do in a three legged race getting ready to sort out a rhythm to win a very slow race.

Marie put a flat hand on the 'in' door gradually increasing the pressure so that the door opened, every now and again it made a slight creak and they would stop dead for a few seconds to see if anything happened. The whole process was excruciatingly slow and the ladies were getting more and more apprehensive, each of them afraid of different things, but none of them wanting to back out—all for one and all that.

Eventually after what felt like hours the door was wide enough for them to get through. Marie and Steph stood back holding the door so that the others could get through, Matilda first so they could all keep an eye on her, Ashlea followed her and held on to her as she got through. Rosie last, she took the weight of the door off Marie and Steph and signalled for them to start their journey up to the office. They skulked along the left hand side wall which backed on to the alley and it was pitch black, the only tiny glimpse of light was from the staff room window and that was obscured by books from where they were creeping.

They could occasionally hear subtle noises while the other ladies found their hiding places and a creak as Matilda sat on a small chair. As they neared the back of the library they could hear low level noises coming from the kitchen, a scrape here and there and the sound of the tap.

They split up once they got to the same level as the door to the office. Marie squeezed Stephs hand in encouragement and smiled a brave smile at her. Steph crossed the library stealthily but without sound and stopped outside the office door. This was the most dangerous part of the plan.

If Darren looked out of the staff room window now he would see Steph and because there was no window in the office door Steph didn't know for sure if he was in the office or staff room, she couldn't risk looking through the window. She needed to go into the office, lock the door behind her then stand behind the office door which leads into the staff room.

She had to hope that when Marie did whatever she did to draw him out of the kitchen; he left via the staff room door into the library and not the door into the office. Well she wanted adventure and excitement and this was surely the escapade that fulfilled that ambition. They say be careful what you wish for.

She grasped the door handle and ignored the lighted window to her left. She slowly pushed the handle down slightly, then a bit more, then fully down—she was sweating profusely and she could hear a buzzing that she hoped was adrenalin in her ears and not a distant chain saw.

Here goes nothing, she thought to herself with bravado she didn't really feel and pushed the door open. Then she waited, so afraid she thought she might be sick. Nothing. Feeling a bit braver and controlling her nausea by imagining what Marie would say if she started retching she walked softly into the dark office. She could see the outline of familiar things there but they looked very different in the shadows; as if they were waiting, ominous even. There was only a faint glimmer of light from under the door leading to the staff room. She took stock of the room in her head and let herself sense where everything was, she couldn't take the risk of tripping over or bumping into something. She took a careful step forward but jumped and almost backed out when she heard the clang as something metal crashed in the kitchen—Darren must have dropped something. Steph stayed where she was with the door in her hand, pulling her breathing back down to a rhythm that would keep her conscious. Smoothly and cautiously she closed the office door, taking what seemed like hours to allow the handle back up.

There was some activity in the staff room and cold fear seeped through Steph, she began to feel dizzy and could feel panic rising in her chest; until she realised she had stopped breathing. As soon as she took a slow quiet but deep breath, she started to feel better. She slowly moved away from the one door and towards the other. She stood still right in front of it and waited for a divine message to help her through the next few minutes.

Marie waited in the shadows of the origami and paper folding section of non fiction until Steph had closed the office door. She had to do something to draw Darren out and give herself the opportunity to try and speak to him before the police got here. She carefully pulled out a huge craft book held it out in front of her, and then dropped it.

The noise was phenomenal and the echo of it seemed to go on for hours, the whole building seemed to reverberate with the noise and she heard a gasp in the book stacks. For a couple of seconds it's as if the whole world was frozen and time stood still. Then the staff room door opened. Marie heard another sharp intake of breath and realised it was her—she slapped her hand over her own mouth.

She heard Darren take a couple of steps out into the library. She could see his shadow cast by the only light in the building, in the room he was leaving. Her heart was beating so hard it was thumping in her ears; she was worried that it was so loud he would hear it. She waited, mentally urging him to let the door close behind him. He took another step and let go of the door. This is it, thought Marie, time for action.

She heard the gentle click as Steph went from the office to the staff room and she actually felt a trickle of sweat slide down her spine. Then the clunk click as Steph locked the door.

She saw the shadow move back and try the handle of the door; he rattled it fiercely "Oy, who's there. What's going on?" A bang as he slapped the door, frantic now to get back in. "The door is locked Darren, you can't get back in" Marie said quietly. As she spoke she moved to a different area. "We know you're creating drugs in there Darren and we don't like it." "Who the fuck is that?" Darren said loudly but not shouting, his shadow starting towards where Marie was standing when she spoke. Marie worried about the language upsetting Matilda, but carried on, moving to where Darren was standing originally "We know you killed Barry, but we don't know why"

She continued in the quiet but controlled voice she had chosen for this exercise. She had created a character for herself to do this interview and even her facial expressions were carefully chosen to give her artificial confidence in herself.

"You're off your head love—I'm just the cleaner, I didn't kill no one." He frowned in the half light trying to see where she was. "I know your voice—I know who you are now. One of the interfering old bats who works here. Which one are you? What do you want?" Marie was unhappy with the description but felt it wasn't the right time to challenge him on his perception. "It doesn't matter who I am" she was quietly moving after each sentence, watching his shadow to see which way he went. "The important thing is why I am here and that is to get answers for your murder victim. Why did you kill poor

Barry?" "How many times do I have to tell you? I didn't kill anybody. What makes you think it was me?" He was speaking huskily now as if he was afraid of being overheard.

Marie could see him walking back towards the staff room door. "Barry's ghost told us where his body was and his ghost gave us the clues which lead us to you. So you see, our witness is very reliable." Darren burst out laughing sounding relieved "You're all fucking barmy. A ghost told you? I can just see that standing up in court. Look love, I'm going now. You can't prove I was ere and you can't prove I killed your Barry" he started walking more quickly down the library. Marie rushed out so that she was a few feet behind him and he could see her "Darren" she called levelly still in character.

He stopped and turned round definitely more confident now. "You took a bit of a risk didn't you love, coming here if you believe I killed your Barry? Who's in the office? What is it you really want? How did you know I was here?" He took a step towards her.

"Stop where you are young man, I'm the one asking the questions. My accomplice is in the office and the doors will remain locked until you have given us the answers we need." Darren laughed again "You think you're CSI don't ya? How do you think you're going to get a confession out of me? What's to stop me walking out of here? Better still I could knock you out cold, kick the fucking door in and knock your mate out, get my stuff and leave here for good. Don't think you could stop me eh love?" He sounded menacing and was getting louder and more confident. Marie's heart started its loud pounding in her ears again.

"The games up for you Darren you might as well confess." Even to her ears she realised she sounded like a teacher rather than someone a criminal wouldn't want to mess with, which was the approach she was trying for. Not for the first time that night she wondered at the wisdom of this barmy escapade.

CHAPTER ELEVEN

He started walking determinedly back up the library towards Marie and she froze. As he got to one of the intersections between the shelves, a large pink apparition stepped forward into his path—he squealed and dropped to the floor in a heap. He was rocking and making a moaning sound with his arms and hands fully covering his head. Matilda looked back at Marie, puzzled, she accepted it was dark and she had made him jump, but this extreme reaction seemed a little over the top.

Of course Darren didn't know she was there and had just been told a ghost had given him away. And brave though he acted, the next thing he new a large pink apparition materialized soundlessly in front of him—it was understandable he was petrified.

"Oh God leave me alone. I'm sorry, really sorry. It was just an accident" Mumbled Darren from inside his arms which were still covering his head. Marie's ear's pricked up any fear temporarily forgotten.

"An accident? So you admit it, you killed Barry?" she demanded excitedly.

He slowly looked up out of the safety of his arms. At first his expression showed that he was terrified, but that melted to a nasty smirk when he realised that Matilda wasn't a ghost. He grunted and snarled through an ugly smile "You got to be fucking killing me! You mad old bat—I thought you was a fucking ghost. You could give someone a heart attack jumping out at people in the dark dressed like that. So its you two is it? I am getting sick of this now" He stood up and started determinedly towards Marie and Matilda. Suddenly a loud bang from behind him made them all jump. He stopped and they all looked in the direction of the noise but there was nothing there.

"Shit. Right you two, unless you want me to cave your skulls in with my bare hands you better get back there and tell your other mate to open that fucking door before I rip your heads off" very aggressive now and definitely not the shy quiet young man he had appeared at the staff meeting.

Marie was a bit scared now and began to regret involving the others in this. She wondered how long they could keep him at bay; they could do with the police arriving now, they were definitely taking their sweet time. She crossed her fingers that they wouldn't have the same mix up as last time and would realise the seriousness of this situation.

Marie and Matilda backed slowly down the library, Marie held Matilda's hand. "You said it was an accident" Marie wheedled carefully. "Perhaps it could have happened to anyone, eh Darren? How did it come about? You might feel better if you talk about it." He sniggered maliciously clearly in control of himself now. "I feel fine about it anyway love, so don't worry about me. Not my fault some old git gets in my way is it? Could have happened to anyone."

He seemed so cold and uncaring that Marie was more determined to find out what happened. "What could have happened to anyone Darren? What did happen?" Her hands were feeling their way along the books and as she reached the edge of the stack she knew they had reached the end of the road. They were at the back door. "What's it to you? You're a librarian not a fucking copper." He snarled "Now get your mate to unlock the door or I'll knock this old bat out first" there was another bang at the bottom of the library. They all turned "Come out now, if there are any more of you. If you don't come out and I find you this old lady pays the price" Darren shouted angrily as he grabbed Matilda's housecoat; he was definitely agitated now. There was movement in the dark at the bottom of the library as Rosie came out of hiding. She stood tentatively in sight but not making any move to join the others.

Darren shook his head in disbelief "This is a joke right, are you all barking mad? What did you think you could do?" He banged heavily on the staff room door

"Open this fucking door now or I will smash your old lady to pieces" he shouted a vein in his temple swelling.

A second or so later there was a click as Steph unlocked the door. Darren motioned for the library ladies to go in before him. "Oy. And you, get in there" he called to Rosie "I want you all were I can see you". Rosie walked slowly up the library and into the staff room; she was trying to kill time until the police arrived. The ladies all gathered together at the far end of the room backed against the craft boxes wall, Steph with an arm round Matilda and an arm round Rosie and Marie in front like a goalie.

The staff room was unusually hot and steamy and there was a strong laundry smell. If they had had any doubt about what Darren was doing before now, they were gone.

On the coffee table was a large white sheet of plastic with hundreds of tiny bubbles in it. About half the bubbles were filled with opaque white liquid. "You lot just stand there and don't speak and don't move. I needed another hour for this lot to dry properly, but I'll just have to risk it because of you interfering old bags". Marie bristled again at his description of them. "Is that right?" she said getting a bit braver in temper. "What is it your dong then?"

Darren looked at her "Nosey you are love—you should be careful, that inquisitive streak could end up getting you into a lot of trouble. You know what happened to the cat that got curious don't you? Don't worry about what I'm doing. You just start praying these are set enough for me to take them or we are going to be spending more time together and to be honest, that's not going to be good for any of us." He had definitely found his feet now and sounded very threatening.

Marie shrugged so pissed off by his constant calling her old she wasn't fearful "Just asking, I'm not really interested in your drugs. I just wanted to know why you killed Barry".

Darren laughed, a mean sound not a happy one. "You've got some bottle love, I'll give you that. Look I meant what I said, it was an accident. He, Barry you said his name was?" Marie nodded "Right, he was coming out of Tesco's and crossing the road towards the library really early one morning.

I had just made a big sale of this lot" he tipped his head in the direction of the tablets he had made on the table. "I got in my car and started off towards home. I admit I was slightly distracted by the big wad of cash I had just collected which was sitting on my passenger seat. There was no cars about, so I started counting it with half an eye on the road. I had seen your bloke when he came out of the shop, but when I pulled off he had disappeared. I thought he must have got into a car, but he had dropped something in the gutter and was bending down, I didn't see him and his head was sticking out into the road. I hit it—his head, with the car."

He shrugged. "I stopped the car, obviously and went out to see what I had hit. I just thought it was some rubbish or something. When I saw it was a man I shit myself. His eyes were half open, so I said 'you ok mate?' and gently tapped him with me foot. He just rolled off the kerb! He was already dead. So I check round to see if anyone had seen me and when no one was about I dragged him into the back of me car." He looked askance at his audience. "Come on, you must see I had no choice? I would go to prison and it wasn't even my fault. Not really, he shouldn't have been fucking about in the gutter when he could hear a car engine should he? I couldn't report it to the police cos of the stuff I had in my car—plus I haven't got a driving licence, so I just panicked. I backed my car down the alley at the side of the library to think about what I could do with the body. I watch crime programmes; I love CSI, so I know they would be able to connect him to me somehow if anyone found his body. Just as I had that thought I noticed the fence and the trees and that in my rear view mirror. It was as if it was a message, so while it was still dark I got his body out and put it on top of my boot. Then I backed the car as far as I could up the alley, climbed on the boot and lifted him up as far as I could and pushed him over.

The noise was so loud I thought the people in that house next door would hear, but no one looked out. To be honest I waited every day for someone to find him, I had almost forgot about him when you lot found him and it was on telly."

Steph sucked in a loud breath "Almost forgot! That you had killed an innocent man and threw his poor body over a fence? And left him there to rot! What sort of a man are you?" she was so outraged she had forgotten to be scared.

Darren raised his eyebrows at her "Whoo hoo it speaks! Did you not hear me? IT WAS AN ACCIDENT. You can't expect me to cry forever can you? He was dead, I couldn't change that, so what was the point of worrying about it? Now all of you shut up, you're giving me a headache." He banged the wall as he spoke his face red, they all jumped and went quiet, Steph pulled Matilda to her.

He went to the kitchen and started collecting his stuff up. He pushed a half a bag of washing powder into his bag and a clear plastic bag of something else white and 2 big spoons. He got a large Tupperware box and came back into the staff room.

He picked up the white plastic sheet and sat down on one of the chairs with it on his lap. He calmly started popping the white tablets out and dropping them into the box.

Marie looked at the others, she was worried about Matilda and was hoping that Ashlea had had the sense to get out of the library and maybe chase up the police.

"Look Darren, shall we just go, get out of your way? We've cleared all that Barry stuff up now, it was obviously an accident.

We'll just go and forget about all this, although it's probably best if you don't clean the library anymore." She started to shuffle the others towards the office door still standing in front of them.

He turned on them with wild eyes. "You must think I'm simple. Stay where you are. I'll be off in a minute, I'll lock you in and leave the keys in the door so someone will come in and find you eventually. Give me your keys" he held out his hand and wiggled his fingers like a grasping child. Steph handed over the keys.

He picked up the white sheet again and rolled it into his bag along with the box of pills. "Pity though, this gig was perfect for my little project. I quite enjoyed cleaning the library while they were setting too. Therapeutic. If I wasn't such a peaceful guy I could be really mad at you lot for spoiling my business. Lucky for you I'm due a holiday anyway." He swung his bag up onto his shoulder and picked up his coat which had been slung across the other chair. He checked the office door; it opened. He locked it. He walked to the door into the library and opened it. He looked back at them as he walked through it and smiled a self satisfied grimace, then he closed the door and they heard it lock.

Marie dropped to the floor with her head in her hands. "Oh God I hope Ashlea stays hidden" she looked up at the others and gathered her wits. "Ok ladies, not exactly as I planned it but we did get the confession. Matilda sit down hun, you look like you might topple over." She raised her hand to guide Matilda into a chair and stood up herself. "Everyone ok?" she asked in a mock cheerful voice? She went to the door and just as she reached it they all heard a scream.

Marie moaned, a pain she couldn't describe was constricting her heart and she could feel vomit rising in her throat; she grabbed the door handle prepared to rip it off to get to Ashlea.

As she looked out of the window, she saw Darren's back, slowly moving in reverse towards the staff room. "He's coming back? He's coming back. Oh no, what could have happened?" She herded Steph and Rosie to where Matilda was sitting "You can either sit there or you could go into the toilet? You could lock yourselves in" she whispered hurriedly trying to gather them all up in her arms. Rosie looked concerned "What about you? Are you coming?" Marie shook her head firmly "No way, Ashlea could be out there, if I can get out to her I will." They realised it was too late for any of the ladies to hide as they heard the door being unlocked. Strangely Darren was still facing away from them; they could see the back of his head through the window in the door.

The door opened slowly, the ladies were too intrigued to try to hide. Darren walked backwards into the room, slowly and carefully taking each step. Marie held onto the door to keep it open and the ladies looked into the library squinting to see what was forcing Darren backwards. In the dark they could just make out Barry floating on the other side of the doorway. No expression on his shimmery face, no eerie pointing of a ghostly finger, just complete blankness.

But it had scared the living daylights out of Darren, he was completely white and his expression was a frozen scream mask, well almost.

They all crowded round the doorway to see what was happening just as they heard Ashlea say "Excuse me" and she walked round Barry, giving him a wide berth. She stood in the doorway with her hands on her hips, all business. "Are you all ok? I was so scared when he took you in there; I thought he was going to shoot you or something. I didn't know what to do. I went out to phone the police again and they said a car was on its way, but I was too scared to just wait so I came back in and sat on the floor and started saying 'Barry Thomson, Barry Thomson but I thought he wasn't listening so I just said 'Barry if you're still here I need you now cos the people who have been trying to solve your murder are trapped in the staff room with your killer, so please please come and help me' and he did! Just like that, as soon as I finished speaking he was there. So we both started walking up the library, well Barry floated, just as Darren came charging out, I saw him lock you in and he got a box of matches out. I looked at Barry and he just floated ahead of me and straight in front of Darren. You should have seen his face—I thought he was going to pass out. He screamed like a girl and then froze. As Barry started floating forwards, Darren walked backwards but his face was a picture like a cartoon. I was walking behind Barry but I know Darren couldn't see me" She laughed. Marie grabbed her and pulled her into her arms "Oh princess you are a clever girl! Was it you who was banging earlier?"

Rosie stepped forward "No that was me. I saw how scared Darren was when he thought Matilda was a ghost so when he was coming towards you I threw a book on the floor to try and scare him to try and give you a chance to escape, but it obviously didn't work". Marie smiled at her and pulled her into the hug, "Don't worry hun, thanks for trying. Did you do it twice?"

Rosie shook her head "No, when it didn't work I picked the book back up and tried to replace it quietly on the shelf but because it was dark I missed my aim and it ended up on the floor." They all laughed, "Rosie—we have a murderer in a haunted library with your work colleagues locked in the staff room and you tidy up!! You are classic you really are" Marie laughed out loud hysterically, emotion released now they all felt safe. They all seemed to have forgotten Darren, who was standing perfectly still in the staff room facing the library only blinking no other muscle in his body daring to move.

Suddenly there was a rumble and a bang as police charged into the library. Everyone jumped, but the ladies were immediately relieved, they all looked at each other and grinned widely, touching each other affectionately as adrenalin pumped through their bodies.

It was immediately apparent that Darren was also extremely relieved because as soon as he saw the police he shouted "Help me, I'm here" and started pushing past the library ladies and Ashlea towards the police.

He stopped dead where Barry had been hovering only seconds before. He'd disappeared now, but Darren didn't walk through where he was, he slowly edged round and then ran into the police officer closest to him. He was gibbering pulling at the officer's jacket. "Mad, honestly they're all mad here, those women. Please take me away. There's a ghost, a real fucking ghost. You've got to get me out of here; he's come back for me. It was a fucking accident! I didn't mean to kill him; he was the one in the fucking road! What was he doing in the fucking road?"

The police man looked puzzled by Darren and held him by his shoulders away from him, possibly because he was messing up his jacket but more likely because he was spitting as he was babbling. "Son, calm down. I don't know what you're talking about. What was an accident? What's been going on here, who's come back for you?" The PC looked genuinely perplexed but from behind him Sergeant Roberts walked up to the group. "Hello there, Darren Mann isn't it? Hello ladies."

He looked from the man to the gang and narrowed his eyes. "I'm not even going to ask what you lot are doing here. I'm too worried about what you'll tell me—especially in front of an audience" he raised his eyebrows knowingly and motioned with his head towards the PC. "But I will be asking you later. You all look like you've had an eventful night so get in the back there and make yourselves a cup of tea while we escort this young man into one of our limousines. I'll have a tea, milk no sugar." He looked at Darren who had stopped gibbering but was totally deflated and still looked afraid of his own shadow. "Come on you, I have a feeling you'll be singing to us for a while. Officer, take young Darren here to hotel Bourneville Lane Police Station, book him in for a single room and make him comfortable will you? I will be along after I have chatted to our super sleuth sisters back there" He gestured to the staff room with his eyes. The PC picked up the bag Darren had dropped when he first saw the ghost and took his arm leading him out of the library, Darren trailing meekly utterly defeated.

Sergeant Roberts had to steel himself to join the ladies in the staff room.

He knew he was going to have to suspend his idea of reality and hold his temper in equal measures. They were irritating, unreasonable and endearing all in one. He took a deep breath and headed their way.

CHAPTER TWELVE

He took the scene in as he entered the staff room. Matilda was snuggled in the office chair, with what looked like a nuns habit wrapped around the shoulders of a bright pink dressing gown as she sipped a mug of tea and listened to the others. Steph, Marie, Ashlea and Rosie were chattering excitedly on the chairs, lap and perched on the table, reliving each moment frame by frame. They stopped when he walked in and looked up at him over their various mugs. They were apprehensive but also felt justified in what they had done. The police had decided that it was easier to write off Barry's death as self inflicted than to find out what had really happened, so they sat backs straight and looked him straight in the eye. Steph got up and went into the kitchen, she came out with a mug for him that said 'flirty at thirty' on it and he wondered how old the mug was.

He smiled at her gratefully "Thanks Steph." Then gently coaching "Now, who wants to tell me what happened here tonight and what you ladies are doing at the library at one o'clock in the morning?"

They looked at Marie, she nodded and stood up self righteous. "We were very disappointed that the police had decided that Barry's death was not murder and that they chose to sully the name of an innocent victim rather than investigate what really happened to him." Sergeant Roberts put up his hand defensively. "Hang on there; we hadn't decided that it wasn't murder at all. There had been a suggestion that Barry may have been up to no good and had fallen and died from his injuries, but that was discounted yesterday. A neighbour came to the police station and filled in some gaps about Barry's lifestyle. It seems that she had not originally come forward because of an incident with a constable and her dog, but felt it was unfair on Barry not to talk to us. Better late than never I suppose. But that made it clear; especially to me that Barry was not a criminal and was killed by someone else." Marie was thrown initially by this revelation and had a brief twinge of guilt that she had not revealed the said information to the police when she had found out this little nugget from Barry's neighbour. She gamely continued "Well that's good. But we never believed that Barry was anything other than a victim and we were concerned that the trail would go cold, so we decided to investigate it ourselves. As you know, Barry's ghost was our man, well ghost, on the inside. He definitely knew who had killed him and he gave us the clues. He floated through the wall to the cleaner's cupboard when we asked him for a clue to who his murderer was. We found out that Darren, our cleaner, also worked at Tesco—there was the trolley coin connection. Finally through doing a bit of detective work of our own, we found out first that there was a local drug dealer cooking up designer drugs and his name was Daz Mann—that couldn't be a coincidence could it? Then we found out that the library appeared to be being used for something at night.

We put two and two together and came up with a stake out situation to find out if it made four! The rest is history." She relaxed back down into her chair, satisfied that she had given a fair account of the case from their perspective.

Sergeant Roberts had forgotten the ghost or rather deliberately filed the memory away and he felt himself become very tense all of a sudden. "So, you're sticking to the ghost story then?" he asked. "It's not a story, its true" Ashlea gushed enthusiastically "He came back to rescue us from Darren when he had mom and the others locked in the staff room. I called him and he came back and floated right in front of Darren as he was just about to escape! He had matches in his hand too—Darren not Barry. I'm sure he was going to set fire to the library, but Barry stopped him dead in his tracks. Go on; ask Darren when you get back to the police station, he'll tell you exactly what I just did."

Sergeant Roberts turned over what the ladies had said in his head, he gently kneaded his temples with his fingers. It sounded so feasible sitting here with them in the middle of the night, no one else around, but he knew when he tried to replay it down at the station it would sound like a fairy tale or the ramblings of lunatics. "Now ladies, I don't want to take any of the glory of the solving of this awful crime away from the er the ghost. But I think it's important to compose a story that explains how this arrest was made without involving the supernatural. Not that I don't believe you, but we don't want to go scaring the community round here do we? You could end up with crackpots from all round the world descending on your lovely little library and you would never know peace again. Now we don't want that do we?" He beseeched them—looking a little anxious.

Ashlea looked at her mom thoughtfully. "He's right you know mom. Half the world will think we're all mad and not believe us and the other half will think we have a special connection with dead people and start expecting us to communicate with them all the time. We could end up with clairvoyants everywhere and people coming down for us to contact their Aunty Agnes. I think we should start at the beginning and every time Barry's ghost is involved, we change the facts slightly so that we stumbled on a clue rather than having the ghost of the victim actually give us the clue. What do you all think?" She looked around, knowing that she was making sense regardless of how late it was and how tired they all were. Steph nodded "You're right Ash, we can't tell the truth, we'll end up in the media for all the wrong reasons and everyone will think we're crackpots. I'll get some notepaper and we can start at the beginning—well, from when Ash came in and told us the police were scaling back the investigation" She stood up to go into the office.

Sergeant Roberts frowned and looked at Ashlea "How did you know that young lady? Only a few officers were party to that decision and it was reversed anyway." Ashlea blushed a bit, not wanting to get anyone into trouble "Mmm, I can't remember now who told me. I think I overheard it in Tesco's" she looked away from the Sergeant uncomfortably and crossed her fingers in her lap. Matilda looked up quite obviously puzzled "I thought you said that nice PC told you on your date" Ashlea forgot that Matilda would no way get that she was subtly trying not to tell where she had got the, clearly secret, information. Subtlety missed Matilda by completely. Marie jumped up and said, a little too loudly "Another cuppa then and some biscuits to keep us going while we write our recent memoirs for the nice officer."

Steph arrived back in the staff room with a couple of note pads and some pens "Feels like de ja vu Daniel, last time you were here we had to write a story based partly on fiction and blurring the truth. That can't be good for a policeman's record" she was only half joking. Sergeant Roberts was offended "Look Steph, you could all write the truth, but do you honestly think anyone will believe you? Darren will be telling the truth and he's likely to end up in a psychiatric hospital. Surely the important thing is that Barry's killer has been caught? And you cleared up the local supplier of dangerous man made drugs. You will all be local heroes. Does it matter that you don't mention some of the facts that might damage the message going out to the wider world? Not everyone is as comfortable with ghosts as you all are. I don't want to make you do anything you're uncomfortable with, it really is all up to you" he put his hands up in surrender, but mentally he crossed his fingers that they would stick with the ghost free story.

Marie smiled at him and patted his hands down reassuringly. "Of course you're right; we can't possibly say a ghost gave us the clues or came to our rescue. Come on you lot, lets start re writing history." Sergeant Roberts smiled, relieved and off the hook "Well, perhaps I had better test out my tea making skills, or maybe hot chocolate would be better if any of us are going to get to sleep anytime soon". He collected the mugs and happily went to the kitchen to make six mugs of hot chocolate while the ladies frantically discussed each stage of the investigation and how they would record it. He looked into the room at them earnestly composing their stories and felt a twinge of emotion he couldn't quite describe. He felt proud of this strange bunch and their dedication to finding justice for a man they barely knew.

They risked their lives and considerably put themselves out to achieve their goal knowing that there would be no reward for them; no one had missed the victim.

Admittedly they had obviously enjoyed the whole escapade, but still he couldn't decide whether he should admonish them for the risk they had taken or praise them for their bravery. Truth is that if they hadn't done what they had done, the crime may never have been solved. Actually it may never have been discovered and Darren would have continued to cook his lethal drugs in the library and sell them to the local youngsters. Knowing this he couldn't bring himself to reproach them at all. The kettle boiled and he set about making night time refreshments for a very eclectic bunch of ladies.

CHAPTER THIRTEEN

Saturday dawned bright and crisp, a white layer of thick frost covering everything and turning even the barest tree and bush into a thing of beauty and worthy of admiration.

Wendy woke up and immediately started worrying about the other library ladies. She reached for her phone. She had a text from Marie at three fifteen in the morning. 'Wend big nite and gr8 result. Library not opening til after lunch so police can get evidence. Everyone ok c u l8r Marie x' She smiled, slowly shaking her head and filling with pride. She had a feeling her friends would solve the whole thing and it looked like they had. She wished she had joined them now. Still she would find out what happened later and she now had a free morning she wasn't expecting. She thought she might bake some cakes to celebrate for this afternoon. She rolled over to find that Mark was already up and then she heard him coming up the stairs.

"I can hear you rolling around so I have come to deliver your tea in bed. I had it all ready with some biscuits as a treat before you head off to work" He was muttering his narrative as usual. Wendy smiled again and expelled a big sigh. She might just stay in bed another hour and have a read of her book, now all this nonsense with ghosts and drugs and murderers was over, she could relax a bit more.

Matilda was wide awake by eight o'clock. She was instantly filled with pride and couldn't stop replaying the moment when she had jumped out in front of Darren and he had dropped like a stone. She kept smiling when she thought about him thinking she was a ghost—he wasn't so brave then was he? She also particularly liked remembering the bit when he backed into the staff room with Barry shimmering in front of him, his face frozen in fear again. Serves him right, old bag indeed! The only thing that gave her a real shiver was when Ash had said he had matches in his hand as he had tried to leave the library. Best not to think about the consequences if he had continued with that part of his devious plan. The most amazing thing was that Matilda had returned home at three thirty in the morning, driven home by the lovely constable and Gerald was still fast asleep in his chair! She had had to wake him up and explain the whole episode to him. At first he had been about to get upset but Matilda had just motored on with the story and he got so wrapped up in the adventure he forgot to be cross that Matilda had done something he would consider extremely irresponsible. Gerald had made them a nice cup of hot chocolate and gone to bed and Matilda was fast asleep by ten to four. Gerald however, lay awake wondering how the wife that he absolutely adored could get involved in so many dangerous and bizarre things.

He used to lie awake years ago worrying that one of these days something really serious would happen. He had wanted to protect her somehow, but it always seemed that one way or another she came through absolutely fine. Now he just lay awake wondering in awe about her because he had spent so long asleep on the chair.

Steph woke at nine thirty to a quiet house. She listened carefully in case it was just a pause in hostilities, but she couldn't hear a sound; there was really quiet in the house. This disturbed her more than anything; it was too early for them all to have gone out and too late for them all to be still asleep. She listened carefully and was sure she could hear whispering; this also puzzled her as she couldn't imagine any of her family not using full volume to communicate at all times. Just then the door slowly opened and Nigel peeked round it "Oh you are awake. We were trying to be quiet after your night full of drama; we figured you deserved a lie in after solving the crime of the century."

His head disappeared and she heard him say behind the door "Gilly go and get your moms breakfast tray, the plates under the grill and Genie you bring her tea up" he came fully into the room now. "Are the girls all in?" Steph asked hesitantly. Nigel nodded "Yes why?" Stephs eyebrows did a mystical dance. "I don't think I have ever woken up to quiet when you lot are all in the house. No music, no shouting, no TV, no banging. It feels lovely, like someone else's house, a normal house." Nigel laughed apologetically. "You could be right love; we are a bit of a noisy bunch. But it just shows we can be quiet when we want to and we wanted to today. What you told me that you and your mates had been through last night at the library while I was fast asleep in a chair, made me shiver.

You in such danger while I'm asleep safe in the house! Honestly, talk about still waters running deep! I also realise you are a local hero. I decided we'd better make sure you're fed and watered before the media masses want to speak to you." He looked genuinely proud. The girls came in with Stephs breakfast on a tray and a mug of tea and she sat up to receive it gratefully and felt like she would explode with happiness.

Rosie was woken up by Billie jumping on the bed. Rosie looks across at the clock and was surprised to see it was nine thirty. "Mommy, mommy mommy caught the baddie" Billie was singing to an indistinguishable tune. Rosie smiled as memories from the previous night, or to be more accurate earlier that morning started filtering into her consciousness. Mick appeared in the bedroom with a tray proudly held out in front of him. "Off the bed Billie! I said I was going to wake Mommy up with breakfast not you jumping on her. Sorry Rosie, are you ok? You haven't had that much sleep, but you said this morning you didn't have to be at work till lunchtime, so I trapped the kids in the living room and tried to let you have a lie in. I still can't get my head round you sneaking off in the middle of the night to stake out the library and somehow catch a drug dealing killer! I couldn't sleep at all after you woke me up when you got back. What if something had happened to you? I thought I was the one with the dramatic job, but I can honestly say in all my years as a paramedic I have never caught a drug dealer or murderer and there you are a local librarian and you do just that! Crazy world or what? Any way how are you feeling and eat your breakfast" He grinned at her sloppily, rolled his eyes and kissed her forehead as he plonked a tray of cornflakes and toast and a big mug of tea on the bed next to her. Rosie clapped her hands excitedly.

"Oh how lovely, breakfast in bed. This is the life, I could get used to this, thanks hun and don't worry I feel fine, better than fine actually, I feel full of beans!" She scooped a spoonful of cereals into her mouth and talked anyway although it sounded a bit muffled. "Honestly, I can't believe it myself. I wasn't going to go, I had said I wouldn't be going but then I was here and you lot were all asleep and a bit of me was worried about Marie, Steph and Ash and another bit of me wanted to join in with the adventure. I had already seen a ghost." Mick tolled his eyes again. "I know you don't believe that, but that doesn't stop it from being true. Anyway, I thought, I've already seen a ghost, we faced Darren out at the staff meeting, and I couldn't be too wimpy to see it through and get the confession or make sure the police caught him. It just felt like partly my responsibility to Barry. Just a responsibility as a person to make sure justice was done for a nice ordinary man who had no one else to look out for him." She looked at Mick her mouth a thin line, smiled and scooped more cereal into her mouth.

Mick shook his head in reluctant admiration. "Part of me actually gets that, although I'm sure the police would have got him eventually. But it was just so risky love; you've got two kids here, what would have happened to them if this Darren had got a gun? I can't imagine life here without you." He looked sincere and almost pleading. "Just promise me you won't do anything like it again." He looked down so his emotion was hidden. Rosie swallowed her last bit of cereal and reached for her toast "Well I'm hardly likely to have another opportunity like this am I? Its not like I regularly get SOS calls from beyond the grave, so that's a promise that wont be hard to keep. You're much more likely to be in a dangerous situation than me"

Rosie bit into her toast and sipped her tea with a look that said pure innocence.

Lucy came bounding into the room "Mommy, Julie from next door said to give you this." Lucy jumped on the side of the bed toppling the cereal bowl over, luckily empty so it didn't do any harm, and flung a newspaper at her mom.

Rosie reached for it at the same time as admonishing Lucy "Lucy, don't jump on the bed when I've obviously got a tray of food on here you dope!" She unfolded the newspaper and the bottom half of the page had a picture of her, Marie, Steph, Matilda and Ashlea looking a little tired and straggly but triumphant never the less. The headline said 'Move over Miss Marple, The Library Ladies are Here'. "Oh my goodness, we're in the paper" she lifted it up for Mick and the children to see. "They took this picture as we came out this morning, but we were too tired to care. Bloody hell we look knackered. Mind you we were knackered so I guess you'd expect it. God I wish I had put lipstick on, I never thought the newspapers would be outside at that time in the morning."

They all went quiet as they read the article. Mick made a whistle "Blimey love, you all sound like courageous daredevils in this story. Is all this stuff true?" Rosie smiled as she thought about Barry's ghost. She had a wan smile on her face as she said "Yep, it all happened like that, we do sound brave don't we?" The phone rang before anyone could say anything and Billie shot out of the room to get it. He came charging back in "It's for you mom" and flung it onto the bed for Rosie in an attempt at an overarm cricket bowl. She rolled her eyes at him and reached out for the phone. "Hello, Rosie speaking" she said in her sing song telephone voice.

She listened for a few seconds then she shook her head "No honestly, I don't want the day off, we're not going in until after lunch anyway because the police were collecting evidence, so we'll be fine." She pulled a funny face at Lucy and Billie while the person on the other end of the phone call apparently spoke. "No honestly, I can't speak for the others, but I definitely won't need counselling. I'm sure that spending time with the others and talking it over with them will be enough for me." She raised her eyebrows unnaturally high and wobbled her head. "Yes, I have a very supportive family. Mmm, ok well thank you for that and see you on Monday, Byee." Rosie cut the phone off and passed it to Billie. "Put that back for mom there's a good boy. Well, you know you've arrived when the regional librarian is coming out to see you! She's coming to visit us all on Monday to show her appreciation for our bravery in tackling this issue. Hilarious, she offered me counselling and said I didn't have to go in for a few days! No chance, I want to relive this every day until I am sick to death of it. Now it's over, it's the most fun I have ever had. Mind you, Wendy's going to kick herself when she finds out we could have had time off to recover from our traumatic episode!" Rosie slapped the quilt "Right you lot, thanks for my breakfast in bed now clear off, I want to get showered and up and ready for work. Chop chop" she clapped her hands as she said this and shooed the children out. She winked at Mick as she jumped up and skipped off to the bathroom.

Marie woke up and was facing the window; she admired the beauty of the tree outside, bare branches but covered in a thick layer of frost which had tiny white spindles dripping off them giving them the appearance of a mystical snow sculpture. Then she remembered the night before and got a thrill in her stomach that made her giggle out loud.

She looked up at the clock and it said ten to ten. Lovely she thought, a nice lie in, but she was wide awake now. She burrowed into the pillow with her head and pulled the quilt up to her chin ready to relish her memories.

Just as she was up to the part where she is climbing through the half opened library door, she had to get up to go to the loo. She flushed the chain and as she was washing her hands she heard Merch coming up the stairs. "Hey there Poirot, are you coming down? I have made your tea" He pulled a cute face which always got him his own way. Marie thought for a minute and wished she had held on to her wee for another fifteen minutes so she could have relived a bit more of the adventure in peace first. She sighed "Ok, I'll just get my dressing gown and come down".

She went back into the bathroom and caught her reflection in the medicine cabinet mirrors. She looked more tired than she felt and one half of her hair looked like a feather duster, but she smiled at her reflection and thought 'We did it. We said we would and we did. For Barry.' She walked lightly down the stairs and into the lounge where Merch had laid out cereals with banana chopped on top of it and a mug of tea next to a small plate with digestives on. Marie shook her head happily "You barmpot. Thank you this looks lovely." Merch waved an arm as if he was a medieval servant and bowed low. "Nothing is too much trouble my fair lady. When you told me about the stake out last night, I don't now what I thought you were going to do. I was just humouring you, I never thought for a minute that this Darren was actually going to be there cooking up drugs and admitting to killing the other guy. I still can't believe it either, but I know it's true. Apart from you telling me this morning, Danni phoned me earlier to say you were in the paper!

I will get some copies while you're at work—are you sure you have to go in? Couldn't they give you a day off?" He asked hopefully. Marie shook her head with her mouth full of cereal, swallowing in time to say "No way, I wouldn't have the day off if they offered! I can't wait to get in and talk about the whole thing with the others. Wendy's going to kick herself that she missed out. Oh and there will be people coming in all afternoon to talk about it. Its so exciting, nothing like this has happened to me before!" Merch looked perplexed "Nothing like this has happened to anybody before! You really are mad." He shook his head again and lifted the empty cereal plate up to go into the kitchen.

Marie picked up the mug and plate of biscuits and made her way upstairs to have a nice refreshing shower and wash her hair; she wanted to look her best for all the attention she imagined the library ladies would be getting.

CHAPTER FOURTEEN

Marie text Steph and Rosie 'Cant wait til one going in at 12.30 if u come early ill bring chips x' Steph text Marie and Rosie 'Me 2! Ill bring choc biscuits x' Rosie text Marie and Steph 'Me 3! Bringing cake x' Ashlea text Marie 'mom wat time u goin in? I wanna com in 2 chat—still buzzin ☺ x' Marie text Ashlea '12.30 4 a picnic c u there xx' Daniel text Marie 'Date went really well how was the stake out? Xx'

CHAPTER FIFTEEN

The library ladies and Ashlea all arrived at the library at just after twelve fifteen. Rosie pulled up outside the library first as Ashlea was running down the hill. "Rosieeee, wait for me!" she shouted, panting loudly. Rosie looked up at the red Ashlea and laughed "You are too young to be out of breath just running down the road from your house." She carefully avoided the speeding Ashlea as she tried to stop and not knock the box full of cake Rosie was clutching to her chest with one hand as she tried to lock the car door without dropping it.

Just as they reached the bottom step Marie rounded the corner in her car followed closely by Steph. They pulled up together as Wendy walked across the road from Tesco. "So hello there super heroes! I though you would all have your pants on the outside of your clothes today a big 'S' on your chests" she was smiling happily and had a box of chocolate fingers in her hand.

"Damn! Knickers—I knew I had forgotten to put something on" Marie pretended to slap her own head "Plus with this chest I'd have needed an S on each one and SS doesn't give out the right message". She leaned into her car and picked up a big carrier bag with 'A Chip off the Old Block' filled with tempting smelling chips.

They all climbed the stairs and Steph unlocked the shutter "Amazing to think how we had to undo this last night! All silent and dark like cat burglars but more scared and less agile. Seems like a dream already now."

She wound the shutter up and put the key in the door turning it as Gerald and Matilda pulled up. They could see Matilda speaking to Gerald as she got out. More unusually Gerald turned off the engine and got out of the car; he padded round the car in what looked like slippers in the shape of Homer Simpson. He stopped pointedly and put his hands on his hips "So, here we are then, the scene of the dastardly drugs drop drama and ghostly apparition aided apprehension of an accidental killer.

I bet you're all very proud of yourselves today aren't you?" The ladies all looked at each other, not knowing if they were in trouble or not. "Well I happen to consider you brave and stupid. See you later Matilda". Gerald promptly got back into the car and drove off without a backward glance.

Matilda grinned widely at the others "Well, we've clearly impressed Gerald!" and started up the steps to the ladies waiting at the top who were looking decidedly confused. "Really?" asked Ashlea "that's demonstrating him being impressed?" They all followed Steph into the library. "Oh yes" said Matilda gravely "he wouldn't have got out of the car in his favourite slippers unless he was very angry or very impressed" she nodded her head slowly to show how serious this evidence was.

"And you could tell from his comment that he was impressed and not angry?" Ashlea continued eyebrows rising suspiciously. Matilda gave Ashlea a little push and laughed "Oh you are funny Ash" and carried on into the library. Ashlea looked at Rosie with a very bemused look on her face and Rosie shrugged and linked arms with her to go inside. Wendy went in last and locked the door behind them.

The staff room was lovely and warm and smelt of fresh laundry. Wendy made a big point of sniffing the air "Oh I love the smell of fresh laundry, makes me feel so clean and fresh." She had a faraway look on her face and her eyes half closed.

Marie, who had started dishing out chips onto an odd assortment of plates, burst out laughing, followed by Steph, Rosie and Ashlea. "Oh Wendy, that's the smell Darren left behind from mixing his drugs with laundry powder! He boiled water and added all his concoction together and put them into tablet shaped plastic there on the table to set. They were there when we came in here last night" Rosie pointed to the table shaking with laughter. Wendy's eyes opened sharply and she pulled a disgusted face "Oh no, I will never enjoy that smell again! He's ruined that smell for me now. Thank goodness it's being taken over by that lovely chip smell. Here, pass me those plates." She leant into the kitchen and started passing out the chips to the others gathered in the staff room.

As usual it was squashed in there with all of them eating, but no one seemed to mind; Matilda sat on the office chair, Steph and Wendy on the two ordinary chairs, Marie and Rosie on the table and Ashlea on the upturned book box.

"Come on then—who was the hero of the hour? The story in the paper was great on detail so I think I know what happened; but I think something was missing. Spill" Wendy pushed a small pile of chips in her mouth and waited.

"Barry" said Marie "Barry and Ashlea saved the day at the end. Ashlea called him and he came to our rescue when Darren had locked us in here.

We think he was going to set fire to the library with us locked in but Barry appeared. Darren shit himself—sorry Matilda, but he did, he saw Barry and it was all over." She piled a big bunch of chips into her mouth nodding.

"Actually he shit himself—sorry Matilda, but he did, when Matilda stepped out in front of him in her long pink dressing gown. It was hilarious" Rosie said laughing though her chips. Matilda smiled knowingly, a wise woman disguised as an eccentric "Firstly you don't have to apologise every time you swear, I don't like it too much, but on occasions like this it is appropriate. Secondly, it is a housecoat and you are right, he did s.h.i.t. himself when I stepped out. Every time I think about it it makes me laugh" she held her hand up to her mouth like a naughty girl and the other ladies laughed even more.

"Really Matilda!" Admonished Wendy pretending to be outraged. "I'm surprised at you; scaring young men half to death in your nightclothes and then swearing about it. And what were you doing out at night in your dres. housecoat?" she popped her last mouthful of chips in and stood up to collect everyone's plates.

Matilda was clearly relishing her moment of glory "There was a stake out for me to join and I didn't have time to get dressed therefore I called a taxi from the upstairs phone when I was supposed to be going to bed so Gerald didn't know I had gone out. He wouldn't have let me come. I know it was naughty but I just couldn't miss it. For Barry you see."

They all nodded. "For Barry. We got justice for Barry. We need to have a service for him now. I bet he's gone already, settled down into wherever he was headed" Rosie tilted her head in a wistful manner as if she was going to miss his visits. "God blimey I bloody hope so! That's enough adventure and haunting for one winter thank you!"

A blast of air which blew through the room alerted them that something was out of the ordinary. They all went quiet and looked to the doorway by the kitchen. Sure enough Barry was standing there, all see through and shimmery. He just floated there, no smile no wave, nothing. They didn't know what to do. Rosie leant down towards Marie "What do you think he wants? Shouldn't he have 'passed over' or whatever by now?" Marie shrugged "Just because I found his body doesn't mean I am a Barry expert. How do I now what is supposed to happen or what he wants?"

Matilda stood up "Now Barry, shouldn't you have gone on somewhere now we found your body and solved your murder mystery?" she said as if she was telling off a small child. Barry nodded slightly.

Matilda put her hands on her considerable hips "Well? What do you want then" Barry didn't move. Matilda scratched her head like a cartoon puzzled person "Do you want anything else from us?" a second or two later Barry shook his head. "Well, did you want to say thank you or good bye?" Barry's shimmery mouth slight curved up in a hint of a smile and he nodded. Matilda used a no nonsense voice to say "Well, you've said it now. You're welcome Barry, we can't bring you back but hopefully you can rest in peace now. So off you go and good luck." She waved her hand at him. The others waved hesitantly too. He kept the almost smile on his face as he gently floated up through the roof of the library.

Matilda looked around at the silent ladies, all of whom had tears in their eyes. "Come on girls, we did a good thing. Barry got justice because of our actions." She paused significantly and took a deep breath. "Now Rosie, get that cake out, I'm ready for pudding". Ashlea giggled and said "Matilda, you make me laugh, you and your food—nothing can upset your stomach can it? Not even your ghost" Matilda patted her on the head like a small child she was indulging "Not my ghost dear".

Rosie opened her Tupperware box and reached in for the magnificent looking chocolate cake. She placed it on the lid and fetched a knife from the kitchen and some kitchen roll (to save the washing up). She sliced it up evenly and placed a slice on each sheet of kitchen roll and passed it to the friends in turn.

"Lets have a cake toast; To Justice for Barry and brave library ladies." They all said 'here here, Justice for Barry' and pretended to tap their cakes together.

Marie, as always was first to take a huge bite and expelled a muffled "Mmmmm" at the same time as Steph said "Rosie –what's in the cake with the chocolate hun?" wisely asking before she bit into it. Rosie cracked a very cheeky smile "Peas! Honestly I can't believe I didn't think of it before! At about five o'clock this morning I woke up and though 'peas and chocolate—the perfect combination' it's the mix of texture that will make it work and as soon as I got up, I made it. What do you think?"

The End